# A Week in the

# Miserable Life of

# Lloyd Canard

## Adam Kirk Pruden

# A Week in the Miserable Life of Lloyd Canard

ISBN 978-0-9843355-2-7

## About the Author

Adam Kirk Pruden grew up in the itsy-bitsy town of Roxobel, North Carolina. After barely graduating from Bertie High School he entered the Marine Corps with the expectation that he'd never have to go to school again. Six years later he found himself without a job and faced employers seeking to hire only college graduates. In frustration he commenced night classes and only eight long years later graduated with a master's degree in business management. To this day he still has never worked in the field. Pruden credits his more than twenty years of government service for exposing him to a multitude of fascinating people and an assortment of amazing experiences which have continually generated new ideas for his stories and characters.

http://www.UniToad.com

# *** DAY ONE ***

# Monday

Lloyd Canard was just one among several thousands of motorists traveling highway I-595 on the daily commute to work in Fort Lauderdale, Florida this Monday morning.  Much of the local South Florida population was comprised of rude, angry people and now here they were, suffering exhaustion and overindulgence from the weekend, amassed on this overburdened strip of freeway with the uninspiring task of returning to the torturous routines which they revoltingly referred to as 'work.'  While Lloyd was rarely the type of person to be noticed in a crowd, he did differ greatly from the many other drivers on the road this morning.  It is true he was gloweringly at odds with the yobs because of his driving precision; he actually obeyed the speed limit, employed turn signals, drove in the proper lane, never passed on the right or utilized the exit lane or median to overtake another vehicle.  But Lloyd Canard stood out most significantly in a manner that you could not know from a quick glance: his attitude.  Mr. Canard was unlike the great majority of his fellow commuters simply because he was happy to have finally made it to Monday morning and be returning to work. He longed for Mondays because it meant he had the full work week to look forward to.  He was relieved that the dreadfully slow weekend was finally over and he was thankful to be returning to a place which on some rare occasions he could exert a little authority or possibly find a brief bit of solitude.

He spotted a car on the side of the roadway up ahead with a very obviously distraught woman crying precariously on the curb in apparent oblivion to the dangers of the raging morning traffic. As usual, he was running behind schedule and needed to get himself to the office without further delay.  But whenever he passed a stranded or disabled motorist, he always let it bother him for hours and sometimes even days.  He had no greater desire to be a hero than any other equally below average adult male but for some reason, which he himself was unable to comprehend, he would hold himself responsible for not providing assistance and his conscience would beat him up for missing the chance to make a positive difference where he might have.  On his worst days dealing with this self generated guilt was even more difficult because he really didn't feel he had much of anything favorable to focus on in his whole life.  His days at work were long, aggravating and devoid of any professional or emotional reward.  His evenings at home were even less enthusiastic.  And he didn't even have the benefit of any hobbies to use as distractions...unless you counted his frequent episodes of daydreaming; but that was more of a coping tool really.  If he could just do one good deed, sacrifice a few minutes to make someone else's day a little better, then he imagined that he could thrive on that positive feeling for days and possibly even for weeks to come.  He even felt better just for thinking about it.  What if this lady was really in distress?  What if the unfortunate woman just happened to be the friend or relative of someone of importance, with authority or even a celebrity?  His unselfish offer of roadside assistance might unleash a chain of events that could lead to an entire change of his life's path.  He would be a hero, bearer of a face that is recognized by the appreciative masses, overwhelmed with offers to buy lunch, coffee or a beer.  With a freshly adopted spring in his step he may receive a newfound respect from others, a better job, a new wife...BAAAUUUHM, BAAAUUUHM!!!

"What the hell?!" he screamed out loud in his empty car. He was abruptly awakened from his dream of grandeur by the deep blasting horn of the eighteen-wheeler that was barreling down on his rear bumper.  The loud, low tone vibrated within his bones and quickened his pulse as Lloyd's meandering mind was cruelly pulled back into its awful reality.

"Damned psychotic drivers!" he exclaimed in retort as he quickly flashed his eyes from his rearview mirror to his speedometer.  Lloyd saw that during his blissful ponderings of hero-hood he had eased his foot from the gas and reduced his speed nearly fifteen miles per hour slower than the pace of the other clearly more aggressive, morning commuters.  Shaken from his stupor and realizing the fault was actually his own, he accelerated quickly and looked up again for the lovely, disabled motorist. But she was no longer there. Not a trace remained of her or the vehicle; it was as if she had been a ghostly apparition that for some mystical reason had chosen to reveal herself only to him.

"Wow, what an incredible experience!" he stated out loud as he thought to himself that maybe he really did have a special purpose. He then glanced at the passenger side mirror to check the truck on his tail without making eye contact with its driver. That's when the female motorist appeared to him once again. But it was different now. While she was still bawling into the palms of her hands by her car, she was now well behind Lloyd and the distance was rapidly increasing. So he had passed her. In all his glorified daydreaming about coming to her aid and being a hero rewarded with a whole new life, he had become so obsessed with the ridiculous fantasy that he had not only passed right by her, but also probably came very near killing her by creating an additional hazard with his own distracted driving. 'Some hero!' he thought as he let out a sigh of despair. He realized that he was clearly much more of a dreamer than a doer. He continued on his way to work now caring even less about being late as he knew he'd be bothered by this event for the remainder of the day. Lloyd felt a renewed assurance that today would reach a new pinnacle in the depth of despair to which his life would surely plunge.

It was easier for his sedan to maneuver through the traffic so he quickly put some distance between himself and the anxious trucker. Once having created a cushion of comfort, he eased it back down and blended into the regular flow of traffic. Shortly that regular flow became stop and go. As he sat there, Lloyd looked at his reflection in the rearview mirror and thought about how far he'd come from the man he used to see looking back at him. His hair was still mostly dark while only a few gray shoots appeared randomly around the edges of his scalp. His blue eyes were still sharp, although they were accentuated in the corners by hash marks which indicated his forty-four years. He glanced down sadly at his newest addition. While his belly wasn't huge, it was protruding from neglect and seemed to be growing. He had slacked off from a career of daily calisthenics after retiring from the Marine Corps, and the effects of his new lifestyle showed.

Lloyd arrived at his place of work and pulled into the parking lot. He was employed as the Chief of Security for the Bitewoody Executive Center. When he began this job four years ago to supplement his military retirement income it was a small commercial plaza of office spaces and store fronts. The job was meant to be excessively simple and require little effort and less responsibility. He had not foreseen the major changes that would so alter his working environment.

A little less than two years ago the renowned local businessman Lancaster Bitewoody set his eyes on creating something much more glamorous and profitable. Mr. Bitewoody purchased the Jacaranda Trail Commercial Plaza for an undisclosed amount in a deal that seemed to have occurred overnight. Almost immediately construction began on additions and expansions. In an incredibly short period of time the new Bitewoody Center experienced massive growth.

It was now a U-shaped, three-story, strip-mall type complex punctuated at each end of the 'U' with a fourteen floor tower. The west tower held a bank and a variety of business and corporate offices. The east tower housed the casino on the first two floors with eleven floors of the Bitewoody Hotel directly above. The business and hotel towers were actually thirteen stories tall, but floor thirteen was labeled as fourteen to appease those who imagined that particular number to be unlucky. Canard thought this to be a stupid practice which would do more to perpetuate the myth and constantly remind people that they were actually on the 13th floor. But Lloyd overestimated people in this instance and had been proved wrong. He knew that people were generally quite stupid and learned that the same people who preposterously feared the number thirteen could just as well be convinced that the thirteenth floor of this thirteen story building didn't exist simply because it wasn't labeled as such.

The Bitewoody Executive Office Tower, Casino and Hotel was now a grand conglomerate of commercial and financial activity accompanied most appropriately with a large dose of drunken debauchery. What used to be a quiet, conservative business complex operating primarily from 9-5 on weekdays was today a hustling, bustling arena of iniquity twenty-four hours a day, every day of the year. Not surprisingly at all, both Florida senators and a local district congressional representative leased space in the Bitewoody Executive Office Tower.

The expansion of course meant a larger security program and the addition of several dozen employees. The number of security officers Chief Canard supervised had quadrupled. This meant that his duties and problems had twice doubled as well. But Lloyd's increase in both work responsibility and aggravation were never reciprocated in a salary rise. Adding to the volatile mix was the fact that the men and women who most often applied for work in private security were not always the most reliable or desirable personnel. They consisted of high school dropouts with more body piercings than words in their vocabulary; struggling college students with a greater focus on schoolwork than policies; disgruntled retirees who claimed they needed the job, yet felt as if they shouldn't actually be asked to do any work; and police academy rejects who were way too high strung to be confined to the usual boredom of a corporate security guard position. All-in-all they were an eclectic bunch of people with unparalleled experiences and goals that otherwise would never happen to wind up in the same place together. For the most part, the security officers seemed incapable of properly interpreting and following their post orders which had already been rewritten to a third grade reading level; yet they all inevitably seemed sharp enough to very quickly recognize the catchy yet ill-planned initials for the center. Lloyd had given up on breaking them from referring to the center by the unfortunate acronym 'B.E.O.T.C.H.' as it seemed his efforts to abate only encouraged its usage.

Lloyd disliked most of the company's management, his co-workers and of course his mostly useless, good-for-nothing subordinates. But in his defense he actually had real reasons to dislike each one of them. In his mind they had worked hard to earn his contempt, and Lloyd felt like he was only giving them what they appropriately deserved. He wasn't an arbitrarily hate-filled person, and he did not simply hate all people, but rather he waited to get to know them first. He had very fairly given each of them an opportunity to introduce and prove themselves; yet almost without fail they would each find some way to endear themselves to his scorn. Chief Canard had met and worked with a lot of people in his lifetime, and his experiences had repeatedly taught him not to expect very much. Sooner or later they all disappointed him and wound up on his useless idiots list. But despite all these negatives, Lloyd showed up to work nearly every day. He rarely missed work though he spent a good deal of time dreaming of being elsewhere. What motivates a man to keep going to a job he dislikes with coworkers he despises? Truth be told, Lloyd had nowhere else to go. His biggest motivation to repeatedly trudge up to this annoying place on a daily basis was his wife. It may sound quite sweet initially, but the truth is that Lloyd was not so incredibly motivated to provide for her as he was eager to get away from her.

As much as he disliked his workplace, Lloyd liked to come into the office early. His motives were fully personal. An early start gave him a perfect excuse for going to bed early; thereby minimizing the time spent arguing with his wife Perla. As she was never one to rise early, this created his only real private time at home, allowed him to beat the worst of traffic and occasionally provided some rare uninterrupted time in his office.

In the quiet solitude of his office, Lloyd prepared for his day. Checking his inbox, reviewing his calendar, shifting the ever-growing stacks of paper on his desk, polishing his shoes and shining his brass belt buckle were all part of Canard's morning routine. As beat down and without power as he often felt, some of that old Marine Corps pride would still shine through the thick clouds of despair in which Lloyd lived. Something of those lost years still seeped in his veins as he insisted on wearing only authentic leather boots and a real brass belt buckle, which he kept highly shined. Maintaining his accessories provided him with a connection to his past as well as a brief escape from all the craziness that usually surrounded him.

This is where today's first problem arose. He stood behind his desk with his left foot propped on the edge of the wastebasket, employing the use of an old t-shirt to briskly rub a brilliant shine on his brass belt buckle. Just as he was honing the metal to a splendid luster, night shift Security Supervisor Earl Markey was passing by and popped his head into the room through the open doorway, "Good morni..."

Lloyd looked up just in time to see Markey's eyes lower then bug out, followed by his jaw dropping uncontrollably. Markey quickly averted his bulging eyes downward as he blurted a quick, "Sorry!" then turned around quickly and headed rapidly down the hallway and out the front door. Lloyd was confused by Markey's odd action so he followed and caught up with him in the parking lot. Lloyd placed his hand on Markey's shoulder and asked what was wrong. Markey jerked away forcefully and yelled, "Don't touch me!"

Lloyd withdrew his hand and took a step back from concern with Markey's extreme reaction and very curious behavior.

"Mr. Markey," Lloyd asked, "what in the world is wrong with you?"

Markey looked around nervously and responded, "Look here Chief Canard, I know I was wrong to pop in like that, but don't worry, I ain't gonna tell nobody."

"Tell nobody what?" asked Lloyd without any idea what the night shift had done to Markey.

"You know," Markey said, again looking around the parking lot nervously, "what you was doing in there."

Lloyd stared at this man who he was very concerned was suffering some sort of breakdown. Finally Lloyd said, "No, I don't know what you are talking about."

Worried that he would be completely in the wrong to allow Mr. Markey to drive in such a state, Lloyd attempted to place his hand on Markey's shoulder in hopes of guiding him back into the office until he decided exactly what to do.

As he reached out towards him, Markey jerked away and screamed, "Don't touch me! Don't put it on me!"

Lloyd was not professionally trained for dealing with this crazy behavior so he snapped back loudly, "What the hell Earl? Are you sick or on drugs? What's the matter with you man?!"

Markey stared at Lloyd, gazing directly into his eyes with as serious a look as Lloyd had ever seen and said, "Man, I ain't into that. I don't want your nasty hands on me!"

"My nasty hands? What in the world are you talking about??!!" Lloyd inquired curiously, then added, "Earl, I was using a rag on it so my hands are still clean."

"You're grossing me out man!" Markey cried in disgusted despair.

Lloyd stared at the distraught man and wondered what could possibly have upset him so.

Markey finally reached the point where he was done beating around the bush and said, "Mr. Canard, I saw what you were doing in your office and I just want to go home and forget about it.  I promise I ain't going to tell nobody."

Lloyd was thoroughly confused, but had to ask "You mean when I was polishing my...?"

"Stop!" Markey cut him off, "I don't want to hear about whatever you call it."

Markey pleaded, "I don't care what part of your body you want to polish, just close the damned door next time.  Leave me out of it and just forget I was even there.  I just want to go home and forget it."

Finally Lloyd understood the root of this weird conversation. "Oh, Markey.  Oh my God.  You mean you think I was touching my...uhm, touching my...you know...my *self* in there?"

"All I know is what I saw," said Markey, "but I'm going to forget it real quick as soon as you get out of my way and just let me leave."

Lloyd took a deep breath and exhaled with a small forced laugh, "Mr. Markey, what you saw was me polishing my brass belt buckle with an old t-shirt."

Trying to explain Lloyd continued, "I see how it must have looked now, but believe me it was just my morning ritual where I shine my shoes and polish my brass before the big-wigs arrive for all their crazy meetings."

"Oh" Markey answered somewhat cautiously, "okay, well I'll just be going now."

Lloyd could tell that Markey wasn't convinced, but was certain that prolonging his explanation would only make it look as if he was trying to cover something up.  He stepped out of Markey's way and said hopefully, "You have a good day Mr. Markey.  I'll see you tomorrow."

Markey had nothing more to say and quickly jumped into his car, conspicuously locked the door and drove away without making any further eye contact with his boss.  Lloyd had an uncomfortable feeling that this might not be the last he heard of this incident.

It was always the same for Lloyd: people never seemed to understand him and at this point in his life he expected no one ever would.  He pondered whether he was some oddity of nature; visible yet incomprehensible by the mass of idiots surrounding him. Even the sentiment of being besieged by imbeciles caused Lloyd concern.  How could he honestly conceive that he was the only sane person on Earth?  It was probably more realistic for Lloyd to believe that he too was an idiot.  Perhaps if he somehow imagined that he was less moronic than the rest of the population then that might even indicate that he was more intellectually deficient than them all.  Did everyone struggle with these same questions?  Maybe others also felt a sense of disappointment at being the smartest person alive.  Perhaps it was a defect of the human species to allow us to see the inferiorities in others much clearer than in ourselves.  Or maybe this trait was not a defect at all, but an essential survival tool.  The only credible difference between Lloyd's idiocy and that of the turd-brains encircling him was his futile struggle to somehow overcome the inadequacy.  He must have had some hint of consciousness which compelled him to strive for change, yet he was caught like a cockroach in the swiftly swirling surge of a flushing toilet.  Fight though he may, Lloyd was doomed to follow the flow and continue on that downward spiraling path.  These metaphysical ponderings were neither enlightening nor comforting, so Lloyd tried to put them out of his mind and concentrate instead on the workday ahead.

Back in his office, Lloyd tried to forget the weird encounter with Mr. Markey.  Hopefully they could both forget it had ever happened.  Lloyd looked over his daily schedule and checked his email for anything important or pressing.  His secretary, Miss Elizabeth Jordan, came in and dropped a pile of folders and loose documents in Lloyd's inbox, then picked up the much smaller stack of items in the outbox.  She greeted Lloyd with a good morning while she did this paper shuffle, and told him the coffee had just finished brewing.

"Perfect," said Lloyd, "thank you very much and good morning to you Liz."

"You're welcome" Liz sang in her unsteady juvenile tone as she exited Lloyd's office.

Lloyd grabbed the mug off his desk, walked out to the small reception area outside his office and filled it with the fresh coffee Liz had just made.  This space had Jordan's desk, a file cabinet and a small table for a printer they shared.  That was about all that could have fit into the space, but it was sufficient.  He tipped the cup to his lips before telling Miss Jordan "I'll be out on rounds until the morning meeting" on his way out the door.

"You know Mr. Canard, I think I might have like, a sixth sense or something" Liz informed him.

"Really?" asked her boss. Lloyd had intentionally been trying to make a rapid departure for rounds because he knew Liz was prone to unpromising ponderings. He wasn't quick enough today.

"Yeah like," she continued, "I noticed this morning on the way to work like, it seems that accidents always happen around me, but somehow I'm like, always able to avoid them."

"Uh huh" responded Canard in the nicest tone he could muster for something he was totally disinterested in.

"Yeah because like, when I decide to turn or change lanes it always seems that just after I've started to move another car will run off the road, slam on the brakes or just like, start skidding" Liz explained.

Lloyd simply stared at her with a look that he hoped she wouldn't read as anything other than concern. He felt pretty confident that Liz's proximity to so many near accidents was not mere coincidence. More likely they were the results of other driver's being forced to take evasive action in response to Liz's poor driving skills.

"How extraordinary," declared Canard. Then added, "Do be careful out there Liz" as he promptly ended the conversation by walking out of the room before she could continue.

Even with the blabbering and that annoying squeaky voice Lloyd harbored a silly crush on the college student performing an internship as his administrative assistant. It was ridiculous yet harmless as she was half his age and unlikely to have any real interest. Lloyd was careful to mask his feelings and remain professional, though he would occasionally do a little flirting. He attempted to be vague enough to avoid both complaints and commitments. While Liz did not reciprocate, she did endure it all with a cute smile of understanding tolerance. She probably felt sorry for her boss and let him play his stupid, useless game out of pity.

Lloyd's morning routine included the attempt to walk around as much as possible of the Bitewoody Center, checking on all security posts and making his presence known. This was the only opportunity he had on a regular basis to see the night shift personnel so he considered it very important. The Center's large size meant that he usually could not complete a full tour so he tried to vary where he went each time, except for the necessary stop by the first line security supervisor's office which was always his starting point.

Lloyd walked in and said, "Good morning" to the night shift supervisor Ms. Fotheringham who was writing in the official log book.

"Anything interesting last night?" Lloyd asked.

"No sir, Mr. Canard. Quiet and uneventful....just the way I like it" she responded.

"That's great," said Lloyd. "Any incident reports?" he inquired more directly. Any reports generated by security were sure to come up at the morning meeting, so Lloyd always tried to get a jump on it so he could be prepared with the details and to know whether to expect an ass-chewing or not.

"No sir," Ms. Fotheringham smiled, "not a thing Chief."

"Very good," said Canard appreciatively, "thank you Ms. Fotheringham. I'll be making rounds if you should need to contact me."

Lloyd continued on his rounds. Speaking briefly with each officer he encountered, signing the logbooks of each stationary post, asking for reports of any problems or malfunctioning equipment and having a look around.

This early morning ritual was one of the better parts of his day. A quick stop by the posts allowed him to both see and be seen by the officers. Canard often gleamed tidbits of information or discovered broken or missing equipment when making these casual inquiries. From a managerial perspective it was a good thing to do; mingle and talk with employees and give the appearance of being more accessible to the officers, while at the same time maintaining a nimbleness to walk away from a challenging question or problem employee. Meeting them out here on post was always better than being cornered by them in his office. For Lloyd it was also an efficient way to avoid both his direct supervisor Steve Webster and his Assistant Chief Russell Brittle until later in the morning. If he timed it just right and Miss Jordan had the coffee ready, then he could easily carry his cup along with him.

There wasn't a whole lot that Lloyd looked forward to in his dismal life, but his morning coffee was something. Probably the best thing actually; it was warm and comforting yet simple and unpretentious.  It required no coaxing, bargaining or conversation.  Lloyd's recurring dream of being stranded on a deserted island was only hindered by the realization that in such a situation he'd probably have to do without coffee.  Canard was certain that everything else he could easily do without.  It was pretty pitiful that Lloyd's own fantasies fell inadequately short of complete fulfillment.

At 7:45 AM Lloyd began working his way back towards his office.  He wanted to review any new calls or paperwork and refill his coffee cup prior to the start of the 8:15 AM meeting.  This meeting was a daily occurrence.  In all actuality it was not a meeting about anything in particular.  He thought the whole idea of meeting around a conference table with six to eight people all staring at each other to see who had anything relevant to say was a big waste of time.  In his point of view, a meeting with a purpose was fine and might possibly have a chance of being even productive, but a meeting just because it was 8:15 AM was quite silly and actually hampered efficiency.  Any positive outcome from these daily meetings was purely accidental, coincidental, uncalculated, unintended, unexpected and an absolute surprise.  Very little else seemed so well synchronized in Lancaster Bitewoody's Business Complex, but oh could they hold a meeting!

He had tried on several occasions to get this point across through small, indirect comments, but the big boss just didn't catch on and Lloyd chose not to pursue it too much as the President and CEO, Mr. Bitewoody, seemed to really get some odd thrill from his daily appearance in front of the heads of each department.  Canard thought CEO Bitewoody was reluctant to end the routine meeting because he so desperately needed someone to talk to and this unfortunately captive audience was the best he could evidently do.

Once everyone had gathered around the conference table, Mr. Bitewoody took his seat and all conversations and morning greetings ceased.  Mr. Bitewoody began by looking directly at Lloyd and saying, "Mr. Canard, please tell us about what happened last night."

Lloyd had an uncomfortable feeling that he was looking for something specific, but since he had applied the foresight to see the night shift supervisor Ms. Fotheringham and received her assurance that nothing had occurred, he replied in what he hoped was a confident tone, "No reportable incidents and nothing out of the ordinary sir."

Bitewoody smiled. It was one of those tight-lipped, clenched-teeth smiles which immediately reveals that you've been caught. Lloyd's confidence ran out the door as his heart did a belly-flop from his chest into the pit of his stomach. The CEO sat quietly for a moment allowing the tension to build. His headful of tight, white curls shone brightly from the spotlight underneath which he sat. Then he spoke: "I want to know about the baby."

Lloyd was totally caught off guard and heard himself stupidly repeating the words, "about the baby..." before catching himself and saying, "I'm sorry Mr. Bitewoody, but I have not been informed of anything regarding a baby."

Lloyd caught the eyes of Casino Manager Giovanni Bigglio sitting across the conference table from him just as Giovanni grimaced and mouthed the word, "Sorry."

"Is that right?" Bitewoody continued with a twinkle in his eye.

Lloyd could tell that his boss was enjoying this moment of superiority over him.

"Well the information I have is that an infant was born on the floor of my casino at 2:30 AM this morning and a couple of your officers assisted with the delivery," Bitewoody served with a smile.

"Oh my God" said Lloyd for the second time this morning "sir, I was not told about this but I will investigate and report back to you as soon as possible."

"I wish..." began Mr. Bitewoody arrogantly as he twisted one of the tips of his well-groomed, solid white mustache, "I just somehow *wish* I could believe that you had a sincere interest in your job Mr. Canard. But the truth is I believe you are one of those employees who only show up for the paycheck."

Lloyd unintentionally locked eyes with Vice President Steve Webster. This brief, wordless interaction distinctly communicated through Webster's harsh look that the V.P. clearly suspected Canard himself had organized this whole embarrassing debacle.

"I'll get right on it" was his only response as he pushed his chair back from the table.

"Yeah, you do that Chief" Mr. Bitewoody said to him dismissively.

Lloyd departed the conference room with his head down to avoid any further eye contact. He knew that his ears would soon be burning as the other managerial staff laughed and joked about how CEO Bitewoody had made him look like a fool once again. He marched directly to the shift supervisor's office and found Ms. Fotheringham on the phone. Lloyd didn't hesitate or wait for her to finish the call before shouting excitedly, "What happened with the baby born in the casino last night?!"

Ms. Fotheringham smiled sweetly as she gingerly replaced the telephone on the receiver and said in a motherly tone, "Oh yeah, that's right. There was a precious little baby born this morning."

"Well why didn't you tell me about it?" he demanded. "I just got sideswiped with this by Mr. Bitewoody in the morning meeting. Where is the incident report?"

Ms. Fotheringham looked confused by his anger as she told him, "There is no report."

"WHAT??!!" he exclaimed. "How the hell can there be no paperwork??!!" "A baby pops out on the roulette wheel, you make no documentation and you don't even think of telling me anything about it??!!"

"Well, first of all," Fotheringham began defensively, "it wasn't on the roulette wheel; it was on the floor by the bar. And secondly, it was a normal delivery without complications, so it really wasn't any kind of incident," she finished confident that she had now put things into proper perspective for Chief Canard. He was astonished. He was unable to speak for several seconds because he could not understand her ridiculous logic. He drew in a deep breath, closed his eyes briefly, and then tried to say very clearly, "Ms. Fotheringham, I need an *incident* report on this *incident* with full details from all officers and staff involved right away. And that means two hours ago. Got it??!!"

"Yes sir" was her simple, unconvinced response.

"Oh and just in case it actually needs to be emphasized further," Lloyd added instructively, "should another baby ever be born anywhere on the premises you are to immediately tell me about it!"

"Brandon" was Fotheringham's one word reply.

Canard looked over his shoulder to see who she was addressing and saw no one.  He looked back at Ms. Fotheringham and she simply stared at him as if waiting a response; like some spoiled dog awaiting a biscuit of reward.

"What?" exclaimed Canard, losing yet a little more control as he lifted his arms into the air to accentuate the question.

"The baby" answered Fotheringham.

Lloyd's face contorted in confusion as his mind twisted around the question of whether Ms. Fotheringham might possibly be a relative of his wife who often employed similarly crude, yet effective methods of mental torture.

"Yes...the baby," said Canard a little slower as he tried to remain calm, "I want to know about the baby that was born in the casino this morning."

"The baby's name is Brandon," she responded in an equally slow, measured tone, "you called the baby 'it' several times."

Lloyd's anger was now beyond his ability to rein it in.  "Dammit Fotheringham!" he shouted, "I don't give a damn what 'ITS' name is.  I only want to know what happened; when, where, why and how!"

"We really have to tell you why?" she whispered the question.

"What?" he asked much louder.

"I only asked if it's really necessary that we explain to you 'why' the baby was born," she explained in her demented boldness.  He struggled to ignore the blatant stupidity of that question, and instructed, "I want all the facts, information, times and details in writing, on my desk right now!!!"

He marched out of the room quickly as he was afraid how he might react to another of the supervisor's idiotic questions.  It was difficult to figure out whether she was being insolent or was genuinely stupid, but he decided not to ponder that question right now since it was currently irrelevant.  Of greater importance at the moment was removing his own head from the chopping block and hopefully replacing it with the much denser one of Ms. Fotheringham.

Canard couldn't help but wonder what type of woman would be so unaware of her own physical condition and be so apparently disinterested in both the health of the child and herself to actually have her baby on the floor of the casino bar.  Still, he was glad that there had been no complications and didn't appear to be any reason for the woman to return later with a lawsuit against Bitewoody.  The extraordinary efforts of his normally bungling officers actually appeared to have been proper in this rare instance.

Lloyd already knew he couldn't count on Fotheringham so he wanted to ensure she understood the urgency in this situation.  Like a smart manager he chose to provide her an incentive rather than waste his own time looking over her shoulder.  The perfect motivation for this particular project would come from his Assistant Chief Russell Brittle.

Brittle had no qualms over deriding Ms. Fotheringham for failing to document the baby incident and he stayed on top of her until she had the officers involved complete their reports as well.  As great a burden as he often was to Lloyd, Russ's particular talents were sometimes useful if focused in the right direction.  Brittle usually spoke before thinking, often acted on irrational impulses and possessed no tact at all.  But that's a natural problem for folks like him who believe that they already know everything and that anyone else resisting this truth is simply an anarchistic troublemaker.  In fact, most complaints from officers, other employees as well as the customers of Bitewoody Executive Office Towers, Casino and Hotel were rooted in the continued employment of Russell Brittle.  He was not an easy person to keep on a tight leash, but Canard usually did his best to minimize contact between his assistant and any of the upper echelon management.  As any seasoned manager knows, substandard employees can sometimes be quite useful if employed at the right time and for the correct, albeit limited, purpose.  It was in certain instances just like today when Lloyd could relish in releasing the blunt force of Brittle's minute mind in the direction of retribution against Ms. Fotheringham.

Lloyd finally made it back to his office and Miss Jordan told him she had received three calls from Mr. Bigglio and two from Mr. Webster.  Steve Webster was Bitewoody's vice president over administration and security and therefore Lloyd's direct supervisor.  He was certain they had both called regarding the baby incident, but since he was pretty certain that Webster was *wanting* information and Bigglio was *offering* information it was a simple decision to call Giovanni first.

"Hey Gio," he greeted simply, knowing that if Bigglio had called more than once he was eager to talk. In the dark as he was, Lloyd certainly preferred listening over being questioned again. He was sure that Bigglio would have detailed facts on the incident as he had tremendous resources and was nowhere near as reluctant to share information as the obviously mentally deficient Ms. Fotheringham.

Lloyd collected the facts from Bigglio, received the incident reports from Fotheringham and her officers, added his own little recap in a cover memo and had it all delivered to Mr. Webster by 1:30 PM. Finally having this unreported birth properly documented, Lloyd attempted to avoid his office for most of the afternoon. He would often try to hide at times like these by claiming that he was performing roving patrols, making safety and security checks and visiting the various security posts. One of the few benefits of a poor marriage was that Lloyd wasn't in any habit of eating regular meals. He was much better at ignoring the pangs of hunger than he was at dealing with people, so it was no discomfort at all for him to forgo a visit to the employee cafeteria.

Later in the day, Russell Brittle caught up with Chief Canard and wanted to talk. He honestly had no interest in the conversation, but felt obliged to listen since he'd so recently benefited from Russ's assistance.

"Hey Chief, I wanted to discuss the progress on that physical fitness program for the officers I submitted to you," Brittle began.

"Oh," responded Canard, "Have you made some changes to it?"

"No sir, I haven't made any changes, but I was hoping that you'd had a chance to look at it and see if we could go ahead and implement it for the security officers."

"Well, it's the same issue we've already discussed Russell," he explained, "we can't just throw some new requirement on the officers that was not written into their original contracts."

"But don't you think it is kind of important sir?" asked Brittle.

Lloyd paused as the thought of his own lack of regular exercise crossed his mind, then answered, "That is something that you are most probably absolutely right about Russell, but we haven't the option of doing anything about it at this time."

"Can we at least try to have it included in future contracts?" begged Brittle.

"I don't know Russ," he tried to brush him off lightly. "We'll have to see about that."

Brittle was a rabid fitness fanatic. Sometimes it seemed he had little more on his mind as this was the only policy he ever worked on and frequently proposed to Canard. The only thing the two men had in common was that Brittle too was a former Marine. Russ had been discharged from the Corps for having committed a serious security violation. He allowed media into a government installation without proper authorization. Actually, with no authorization at all, but simply on a whim because the media knocked on the front door and showed him a camera. Bored as he was with his dwindling social life, Russ jumped at the chance to be in front of a camera. Russ was the kind of fellow who exuded confidence: so much so that he exuded it all over those around him in an extremely annoying manner. He was totally self absorbed and absolutely incredulous when others didn't share a similar unfounded admiration for himself. Russell spent much of his time working out in front of a mirrored wall at the gym, cared about buying clothing with gaudily labeled brand names, kept abreast of the so-called news out of Hollywood, California and closely followed what other people claimed was in style. In short, he fit right in with the self-proclaimed beautiful elite crowd in South Florida.

Brittle was his own biggest fan and Canard would not be surprised at the extent to which he might go simply to attract much desired attention from anyone else. His assistant's investments in short-lived material fads combined with his confidence and outgoing flair usually won him a lot of dates with the ladies. Unfortunately, as soon as they had to deal with an evening of listening to him talking nonstop about himself in that annoyingly nasal, high-pitched voice Russell rarely had to deal with second dates. While the outward appearance was that Russell spent time with many different women, the fact was that he couldn't find anyone as equally interested in himself as he was.

Lloyd's hope for a little peace in his office was interrupted in the late afternoon when another day shift security supervisor popped his head in.

Nick Swath announced himself with, "Hey Chief. I just wanted to make sure you got those reports from Norma and the officers."

"Yes I did, thank you," answered Lloyd insincerely. He knew that Swath had no involvement in the incident and his only interest was to belittle Ms. Fotheringham.

"We know how scatterbrained that woman can be about important stuff like that," Swath continued with his effort to develop an alliance, "if you need any help on that just let me know boss."

"Well, everything has already been completed and submitted Mr. Swath, but thanks for your willingness to help. I'll definitely keep your offer in mind the next time something big happens" Lloyd added.

Swath's eyes grew large and his body went rigid as the chief's words struck him with the fear that he might actually be called upon to do some work. "I'll just get out of your way boss, I know you're busy" he added before resuming his normal posture of hunched shoulders and quickly walked away. Even the way he walked, always on the balls of his feet as if tiptoeing to avoid being noticed, matched his wretched personality. Lloyd knew very well that the only reason Nick Swath was volunteering his aid now was because he was certain that all the work had already been done. He was an extremely lazy guy and a complete brown-noser. Though he never actually did much work and somehow seemed to be absent whenever the crap hit the fan, he could always be counted on to show up later and spout strongly opinionated comments on whatever occurred as well as pointing out the errors and inadequacies of those people who actually responded to the incident and jumped into the fray. Ole Nick had decided long ago that he'd make his mark not by taking any action, but by laying low, avoiding conflict and sniping his more motivated peers. It was well-known by all that the only back up an officer would ever get from Swath would be from the tip of the dagger he would eagerly thrust into your back.

\* \* \* \*

It was crazy days like this one that would make a man thankful to have a nice, quiet loving home in which to withdraw, unwind and relax. This type of sanctuary sounded great to Lloyd, but alas it was not at all existent in his reality. Uninspired by the coming of 5:00 PM, and without any anticipation of heading home to his overbearing wife Perla, Lloyd decided to hang around a little longer. He proceeded to the bar in hopes of some anonymous quiet time. He wouldn't mind talking with Bigglio, but Lloyd was well aware that this was the time of day when things really began to pick up for casino operations so his friend would unlikely have time to socialize. Confident that most if not all upper management had departed for the evening, Lloyd slipped from his office and walked to the casino with the idea of having just one drink before heading home.

Ninety minutes later Canard had wasted about as much time as he could and ogled way too many female patrons of the casino. While he'd never caught up with Giovanni Bigglio, Lloyd did use waiting for him as an excuse to have three more drinks than he'd originally intended. Quite a bit more relaxed now, Lloyd proceeded back to his office to close things out for the day, grab his attaché case and head home. Waiting for the elevator, Lloyd felt weary from the long day, but was thankful that it had at least ended smoothly after such a rough start. Now he simply wanted to reach the silence and comfort of his own bed.

When the elevator doors opened a woman stumbled out and bumped hard into Lloyd. His natural response was to extend his arms to prevent her falling to the floor. The unappreciative woman drew back from Canard and reacted extremely negatively to what she interpreted as his rude sexual advances. Although a woman of her age and deteriorated appearance should have shown some gratitude at being merely acknowledged by a representative of the opposite sex, she instead reverted to a defensive response just as she had when the last man made a pass at her two and a half decades ago.

Lloyd smelled the liquor on her breath and took a half step back to create some distance. This woman was way too far gone to remain on the premises. Canard offered her directions to the parking lot as a polite manner of suggesting that she should leave. The rude woman exclaimed loudly, "I work here! You can't throw me out! I have to go to the vault!"

Canard recognized the lady as one of the cashiers in the casino and knew that she had already completed her shift as he had seen her enjoying happy hour in the bar. He also noticed that she still wore her employee badge identifying her as, 'Sharon Demasiado.' Chief Canard was fairly confident that her position did not allow access to the vault at any time, much less after completion of her shift.

Lloyd responded more professionally with the calmly spoken, "Yes Ms. Demasiado. I work here as well ma'am and I am aware that you are no longer on duty and probably should be leaving for the day."

"Get out of my way!" the drunk woman demanded as she reached out and gave Canard a push and attempted to walk past him.

Lloyd stepped in front of her blocking her path and offered a bit more sternly, "Ma'am, I must insist that you leave. I'll gladly have one of my officers escort you to your car."

As Lloyd lifted his handheld radio to call an officer to their location, the woman reacted violently by striking the chief in the chest and attempting to rip the buttons off his shirt. The intoxicated woman's blows were no threat, but Canard didn't want to have his shirt ripped apart so in one smooth, fleet move he grabbed the woman's left wrist with his left hand and using her own arm, pinned her to the wall between the elevator doors.

It was unfortunate that at that exact moment the doors to the elevator on Canard's left opened. The half-dozen people inside stared wide-eyed and open mouthed at the poor cashier being restrained by the big bad security chief wielded a large radio menacingly above her head. Lloyd had not realized that in his swift effort to restrain the drunk woman that his right arm, occupied with the radio, had involuntarily raised itself into what was mistakenly seen by those peering through the elevator door as a striking position. Making things much worse was the reaction of one of the female patrons in the elevator who overdramatically screamed in horror, "Don't hit her again!"

Before Lloyd could respond in bewilderment with, "Again?" he was pummeled and dog-piled on the floor by a couple of large bouncers who were just getting off their shift at the casino. It was evident to Lloyd that their evening on duty had been quite uneventful. The vigor with which they employed this task was, to say the least, overwhelming. Lloyd understood without question that these two overachieving bodybuilders were very good at their job.  He just wished he had had the fortune of downing three hours worth of alcoholic beverages beforehand like the majority of their usual clientele.  They held him prone on the floor with his arms twisted behind him until Bigglio and Fotheringham arrived on the scene.  They walked in at the same time: Bigglio with a grimace of embarrassment and Ms. Fotheringham with a poorly disguised smirk of glee.  Feeling like he'd lost track of time, Canard realized that he'd been at Bitewoody long enough for her to return to work.  He was pretty sure that while Norma Fotheringham might not find a newborn baby on the casino floor worthy of noting, she would most likely not be so tight lipped about the predicament in which she'd just witnessed her boss.

That's pretty much how Lloyd spent his days...centered in the middle of an ever-evolving cyclonic storm of confusion, errors, accidents and misunderstandings.  Such was Lloyd's life and he was not ignorant of the lamentable reality.  He rarely made any attempt to affect events as he had learned long ago that resistance only made things worse.  It wasn't that Lloyd didn't care; just that he knew his efforts would only compound the inevitably convoluted conclusion.  Instead he viewed life like a roller coaster and just tried to stay strapped into his seat while the wild ride continued without his ability to control any part of it.

After the cashier was helped to her car and Lloyd was scraped off the floor he eventually made it back to his office.  He sat down and made a few brief notes on the encounter, but decided to go on home and complete the full incident report early the next morning.

* * * *

Someone said that behind every disgruntled man is a nagging woman.  Perla Canard was a nag, a know-it-all and a nut.  But that was really too vague a definition for the woman Lloyd had married.  Perla was more a bag of mixed nuts.  She stayed at home all day, had not an ounce of professional or worldly experience, yet she was never short on advice to her husband.  Actually it wasn't really advice; that was only Perla's word.  The fact was that it was nothing more than pure criticism.  It was baseless, ridiculous and unfortunately endless.

As soon as he entered the front door Perla blurted, "You're late!"

"For what?" Lloyd asked calmly.

"For to be home" stated Perla.

"To do what?" he asked insincerely.

"What?!" shot back Perla not understanding his meaning, but clearly picking up on his impudence.

"What am I late for?" he slowly asked again.

"Juzt to be home. You too lazy to come on time" Perla responded without really providing a clear answer.

"I got stuck dealing with a problem at work" Lloyd uselessly tried to explain.

"Oh, you work in bar now?" inquired Perla.

"I don't know what you're talking about" answered Lloyd without a clue as to how she possibly could have heard about the run-in with the casino cashier so soon.

"You smell like beer and cigarette" Perla declared.

"Oh that," responded Lloyd, "there was a problem in the casino bar so I was there briefly."

"Yeah, sure" Perla responded just to ensure she had the last word in this foolish conversation.

Whoever said that Hispanic women made great wives must have been under the influence of some pretty powerful substance at the time. Either that or Lloyd had encountered an anomaly during his assignment in Central America. But he had been in his early twenties back then and several years of a largely nomadic military lifestyle had already taken its toll. The young, brown-skinned girl with large dark eyes and hair so brilliantly dark that it glistened in the sunlight caught his eye and completely mesmerized him. The enchantment had lasted long enough for them to marry. But they both still had some growing up to do and since military life is largely incompatible with marriage it meant that they didn't have the best opportunity to experience all of that critically important time together. Too focused on his career and too frequently deployed on military orders, the course of their marriage was determined in Lloyd's absence. Perla quickly became independent and even seemed to develop something resembling almost an aversion to her husband's presence. Left on her own, she had ensconced herself in the unproductive routine which she still continued. Perla Canard was addicted to three things: marshmallows, soap operas and nagging. These three items consumed Perla's life and her expertise in each of these areas was quite copious. She didn't work outside the home and neither did she perform any useful task within. Mrs. Canard flatly refused to cook or clean. Perla's days were filled with hours of lounging on the sofa or in the bed in front of the television set consuming tooth decaying marshmallows by the bag and mind decaying soap operas by the hour. The results of so intense a routine were highly visible in both her insight on the world and her ever-increasing physical presence. Like everything else Perla came up with, there was always some weird, twisted way that it all ultimately resulted in being his fault. In this instance it was that Lloyd had a good enough income that she didn't *have* to work. Her revenge for this defect evidently lay in her plan to spend the money he brought home in a fashion resembling that of an intoxicated young mariner on shore leave with a pocketful of foreign currency whose value he cannot comprehend therefore he treats it like play money.

As Lloyd quietly undressed in the bedroom Perla wandered around like a hen pecking for insects. Her intense focus paid off when something fell with a light 'tick' onto the tile floor as Lloyd unbuttoned his shirt. He didn't even notice, but she dove on it like a hawk after a fleeing mouse. She stood up slowly with something cupped in her hand that she was examining closely. Perla then grabbed the tiny item between her thumb and forefinger and thrust it in her husband's face demanding, "So what's dis?!"

Lloyd pulled his head back to better see whatever it was she held too close to his face. Once his eyes focused he recognized it as a woman's fake fingernail.

He hated trying to explain this, but knew the situation required a response so he said, "It appears to be a fingernail."

"A woman fingernail," Perla stated, "and it fall out of your shirt!"

"Yes, that's what it looks like" he agreed uneasily.

"So, you gonna tell me the truth about her?"

"Of course I am" he answered, knowing full well that the truth wouldn't make a bit of difference in what his wife ultimately chose to believe. He'd spent his life being open and honest, yet invariably suffering for it. It seemed that his calm, straightforward and emotionless delivery was most often mistaken as insincere, or worse; as intentionally belligerent and disrespectful.

"There was an intoxicated woman in the casino and when I asked her to leave she attacked me and tried to rip the buttons off my shirt" he explained quite thoroughly.

"Uh huh," she said, not believing a word her husband said, "so that why your breath smell like beer too?"

"One doesn't have anything to do with the other one."

"Der is anuder one too?!" Perla shouted furiously.

"No, no not another woman," he attempted to explain, "I mean its two different things. I was at a meeting in the bar had a couple beers, then the drunk woman showed up."

"So now you work in a bar?" Perla tried again to catch him.

"No Perla, I do not work in a bar, but there is a bar where I work."

"Well you jus tell jour friend I'm going to keep dis evidence and see what my lawyer say!" Perla declared menacingly before departing the room in a huff.

This was the type of stuff he had to deal with every day. He had no choice but to attempt to explain even when he knew his wife would never ever believe his honest account of what had happened. If a man's home was his castle, why did Lloyd always feel like he was stuck in the dungeon? He suffered Perla's own excruciating version of the inquisition on a daily basis. He knew she'd return for more as Perla was much too fond of arguing and she really felt she had a hot piece of evidence this time. Of course, he knew he was innocent but was also aware that he'd never convince her of it so he was more determined to simply shut her out. One of Lloyd's greatest survival tools was his ability to ignore things. Things included people, bad situations, pain and the random aggravation of everyday life. He couldn't remember when he first discovered this ability. He guessed it was either developed or exposed as a coping tool in challenging or uncomfortable situations. For example, in Marine Corps boot camp he withstood much pain and humiliation because he just wasn't there. It was almost like being outside of himself. He could see what was happening to his physical being if he looked, but the main benefit of the gift was not having to. It was kind of like putting your life on auto pilot and just walking out for a while. While he felt some concern that this special ability caused him to miss out on much of how life should authentically be experienced, he only actually employed the tactic during those times when he knew the experience would neither be enjoyable nor worthy of remembering.

His daughter Andi was a bratty and disrespectful fourteen-year-old kid. Being a typical teenager she usually tried to avoid most interactions with her father. In her know-it-all teen eyes he was just a complete square and absolutely always wrong. Andi seemed to have adopted a disposition quite similar to that of her mother, so Lloyd was frightfully outnumbered by less than congenial females at home.

That evening as Lloyd was preparing for bed he'd left the bathroom door ajar. Andi passed by then slowly backtracked to stare for a moment at her father. Fortunately he had already scrubbed his essentials and was now only washing his hair in the sink. She stared at him in wonder.

He spotted saw her there and said, "Hey sweetie, what's up?"

Andi asked, "What are you doing?"

"Taking a shower."

"That's not a shower" Andi pointed out bluntly.

"Oh, well a bath then."

"That's not a bath either." Then the teenager suggested, "Why don't you just use the real shower that's right beside you?"

"Well, I don't really need a fancy shower with hot water and name brand, sweet scented soaps and shampoos;" Lloyd tried to explain, "all I require is a little bit of gritty, unscented soap and some cold water."

Andi Canard just stared blankly at her father. She had no clue what he meant.

"You see," he now began with an instructive tone, "I'm a man, a real man and a former Marine, so I can get by on the bare minimum. Using hot water and deodorant soap will only run the risk of making me soft and spoiled. You know...I have to keep my edge."

She didn't know. Without another word Andi shook her head and puffed out a mouthful of air to show her disapproval before walking away.

"She's like a little Perla" Lloyd whispered aloud to his reflection as he studied his less than manly-Marine physique in the bathroom mirror.

# *** DAY TWO ***

# Tuesday

Lloyd arrived at the office for what he hoped would be a smoother day, but was instead surprised when his name was called out as he entered the Bitewoody Center's lobby. As much as he longed for them, smooth days weren't usually in the cards for Chief Canard.

The officer on Post One reported that Mr. Webster had left instructions for him to report directly to the vice president's office upon arrival. He thanked the officer for the unwanted message and turned to go to his office. The officer called out, "Chief Canard...uhm...Mr. Webster's office is the other way."

"Yes I know that" he answered quite perturbed but trying not to let it show in his response. "I'll just stop by my office first then head over there."

"But sir," the officer said, now in a more commanding tone, "we have instructions to ensure you go to Mr. Webster's office first."

As Lloyd stared quietly in disbelief he saw the officer lift a handheld radio and whisper something into the microphone. Seconds later two other security officers emerged from a nearby hallway and a third from the stairwell in the corner. He was immediately uncomfortable with the situation: he had no idea what Webster could possibly want that was so urgent and he despised being treated as a trespasser in the office complex where he was supposed to be the chief of security. This was yet another glaring example of just how little respect he commanded from subordinates. Canard had a difficult time getting any single one of them to pay the slightest attention to security details and procedures, but today, as soon as what looked like the opportunity to pummel him for disobeying an order arose, there was no shortage of eager officers swarming about for the chance to manhandle their supposed boss. Canard relented, as he clearly was not being given a choice, and turned to walk in the direction of Webster's office. As he passed the three silent officers providing backup to ensure his compliance he whipped his head around and barked, "Get back to work!" at them.

It was a useless attempt to exert an authority that he didn't apparently have as the officers simply stood in place like statues and continued to follow his departure with their menacing stares. Lloyd was more than slightly disturbed at their apparent eagerness to use force on him. As he walked away he mumbled out loud to himself, "Someday they might just have to haul my ass out of this stupid place by force!" Though he personally doubted he'd ever actually have the balls to follow through with that dream.

Obviously if Mr. Webster wanted to see him this early in the morning there was a problem. He didn't know what had happened last night to encourage Webster to prepare the officers to use force on him, but he'd sure find out soon. Lloyd's body jerked in an involuntary convulsion at the thought of another baby being born on the casino floor. 'Damn,' he wished he could have made it to his office for some badly needed information and coffee too.

Nick Swath appeared from an adjoining corridor and chimed, "Hey Boss, how are you this morning?"

"I don't know for sure yet Nick, but I'm guessing not so well."

"Yeah, that's what I heard" Swath reflected.

"What do you mean?" Canard asked, "What did you hear?"

"Well uhm," Swath stumbled to answer, "you know I don't like to repeat rumors boss."

"Yeah, most people around here really don't like to do that" responded Canard sarcastically.

Swath attempted to change the subject, "So how's your old lady boss man?"

"The same: she's still there" he informed emotionlessly. He was focused more on what Mr. Webster had in store for him. Nearing the Vice President's office Swath peeled away and excused himself with, "Gotta go back to work now boss."

Lloyd said nothing but felt a strong urge to turn and follow him. If there were any well concealed hiding places in B.E.O.T.C.H. Nick was certainly the man that would know them.

Lloyd could read the seriousness from Webster's scowl as he walked in and that made him wish for something as simple as a baby on the roulette wheel this time. Mr. Webster's face was contorted in concern and his shoulders hunched forward as he held several sheets of paper in his hands with his elbows propped on the desk. Canard thought he resembled a cobra coiled tightly in preparation to strike.

Webster began by stating, "Mr. Canard I'm very concerned about this aberrant behavior of yours."

The vagueness of Webster's comment left him at a loss to which of his behaviors he was being chastised for presently. Lloyd stared quietly for a moment as he pondered how exactly to respond. Rather than inadvertently revealing something concerning a yet undiscovered flaw in his character, he said nothing. Since Mr. Webster had not actually asked a question he felt safe in maintaining his silence.

"Well?" Webster finally put forward.

"What are you after sir?" Lloyd proceeded cautiously, "I didn't hear a question."

"Your condescending tone does not aid in this situation Canard" Webster accused bluntly.

"It is actually a confused tone you are hearing sir. I'm completely clueless here."

"I want to know about this letter" Webster said as he emphatically shook the mysterious stack of papers.

Canard immediately assumed that Markey had changed his mind about never mentioning what he thought he had witnessed him doing in his office the previous morning. To make things worse, the blasted man had evidently decided to document his depraved misconception in the form of a letter. Lloyd's anger rose internally, but he attempted to maintain an outwardly calm display.

"I wrote no letter Mr. Webster" Lloyd answered truthfully though less respectfully this time.

"I know you didn't write it, but it's all about you."

Desperate now he tried reasoning, "Mr. Webster, I can assure you that this is simply the result of an unfortunate misunderstanding and is being totally blown out of proportion."

"Out of proportion?" asked Webster with a look of surprise. "You think this sort of thing should be simply tossed off and forgotten?"

Lloyd was disturbed by the double entendre even though he knew that Mr. Webster wasn't witty enough to have said it intentionally. He took a deep breath and tried to remain professional as he reasoned, "Again I remind you that the allegations are completely untrue, but even if it was, would it really require this level of response?"

Webster stared at him in disbelief but said nothing.

He thought it prudent to remind his supervisor, "Besides, everyone does it."

Now Mr. Webster really glared at him as if he were some type of monster.

He immediately regretted making that last statement which probably communicated a little too much to his boss and wrongly labeled himself as a frequent abuser. Deciding to leave the hypothetical and address only the facts, Canard attempted a more thorough explanation to clarify the situation. "Sir, I was only performing my daily ritual..." he paused at this unfortunate choice of words, then resumed with a decision to remain brief, "It was a misunderstanding, Mr. Webster, plain and simple. It was not what it appeared to be."

Now Webster asked, "Well, what was it then?"

"I only wanted to shine my brass belt buckle."

"What?" asked Webster, now completely confused. "How was she going to help you with that?"

"She who?"

"It doesn't matter whether it's a she, he or whatever," Webster caught himself and poorly tried to cover the slip. "I just need you to come clean and tell me what actually occurred and why you did it."

Now even more confounded about what he was being accused of, Lloyd was further irritated to hear that Mr. Webster was already assuming that he was guilty of the mysterious allegations.

"Oh, I thought you were talking about something else" he replied with a small amount of relief as it seemed Markey might not be the author of this secret letter after all.

"Well what else have you done that I do not yet know about?" asked Webster in his falsely authoritative tone.

Thoroughly perplexed now Lloyd tried to explain clearly, "I have no idea what you are asking me about and I don't have any knowledge of this letter you keep referring to." Then he followed with the reasonable request, "May I have a look at it?"

Webster quickly pulled the loose leaf papers to his chest and stated, "I cannot do that Mr. Canard. We are dealing with a whistleblower situation here and there is a protocol which must be followed to protect the individual."

"What individual?" he inquired more befuddled than before.

"Mr. Canard," Webster spoke more sternly, "I have made it explicitly clear to you that I cannot reveal the name of the complainant and risk the possibility that you will retaliate upon her...or him or them."

"Mr. Webster," he began as he stood up, "I do not have any idea what you are talking about and I need to get on with my work."

"You're not going anywhere yet!" exclaimed Webster with a surprising amount of force. "I need a memo from you right away addressing these allegations."

"I haven't seen this letter you are referring to," he explained slowly, "nor been advised of said allegations, so I cannot produce a relevant memorandum in response."

"Your defiance does not bode well for your case. Now draft me a response to this letter immediately!"

Lloyd had no idea what was going on, but was certain that he'd get no useful information from continuing this game with the dim-witted Webster. How the hell was it that the most useless employees always seemed to get fast tracked into management? It seemed to be almost a rule that an employee who should never have been allowed to remain past orientation, and usually created more work than he actually performed, always seemed to be destined for a supervisory role in the organization.

Both as an escape tactic and out of true desperate need Lloyd blurted out, "I really need some coffee." He followed with the insincere offer of, "Would you like a cup sir?"

"Don't attempt to distract me by changing the subject Mr. Canard." "This is extremely serious."

"I'm sure it is" answered Lloyd with a distant, unconvinced look in his eyes. Realizing his only escape would be to play along, he switched tactics. He quickly snapped to attention and gave the desired yet totally fictitious response to his boss, "Mr. Webster, I'll get on that memorandum right away, sir."

"Thank you" responded Webster with obvious relief that further conflict was being avoided. "Your cooperation is very important in cleaning up this matter."

Canard was still clueless as to what the matter truly was, but he could clearly see that Webster had told him all that he was going to. As always, he would have to contact the Casino Supervisor Giovanni Bigglio to get the real scoop about whatever letter Webster was stressing about.

Leaving Webster's office, Lloyd noticed a burgundy beret hanging on the doorknob of the outer door to the vice president's office. It caught his eye as being an unusual place to leave a hat so he casually commented to a security officer walking by, "Doesn't that item look out of place on that door knob?" Not waiting for the officer to answer he followed with, "Rather suspicious, don't you agree?" before hurrying off to find Bigglio, the answers and the sanity he so badly needed.

Chief Canard did not realize what seed he had inadvertently planted in the mind of the young officer. Security Officer Ned Zambrano mistook the Chief's reference to the hat being suspicious as a signal to initiate action. And action to the extreme is what the motivated officer went for. Officer Zambrano contacted the security control center at Post One and informed the officer there that he had come upon a suspicious unattended package. Although rarely the case when a true emergency arose, today the B.E.O.T.C.H. security officers worked like a dream as they began to cordon off the area, evacuate the building and conduct a survey of employees to ensure everyone was accounted for. While things were being handled with surprising precision locally, the state police emergency bomb squad had been alerted and was en route to Bitewoody Center.

As these events unfurled and grew into something much bigger than it ever should have been, Canard was unaware of to what his officers were doing as they never bothered to contact him or inform the chain of command. He carried a radio to communicate with officers, but their decision to keep off the air in the event that radio waves could detonate the suspect device only served to ensure that the Chief was once again clueless about the goings on that he had so innocently initiated and would undoubtedly have to answer for later.

Not surprisingly, Giovanni Bigglio knew exactly what letter the chief was asking about, and even seemed to somehow have knowledge of the complete contents of the mysterious memorandum.  He didn't know how Bigglio seemed to be so perfectly plugged in and could so easily know every little detail of everything that went on in the Bitewoody Center.  But even without a clue as to how he did it, Lloyd was thankful to have Giovanni as a friend and valuable resource.  The two men stepped outside the front of the casino to avoid having other employees listen in.  An observer would find the scene curiously entertaining even without audio.  As Bigglio punctuated his storytelling with the customarily vigorous hand gestures inherent from his Italian background, the chief's face contorted through a series of odd emotional responses.  Even the morning breeze combined with the wild arm swinging didn't produce enough wind to move a single strand of Giovanni's perfectly set, wavy brown hair.

Lloyd couldn't believe how incredibly twisted and convoluted this tale had become as he listened in horror to the stack of lies included in the six page complaint filed by the casino cashier.  When Gio had finished, he stood still; silently thinking how he could respond to such outlandish accusations.  Bigglio was quiet for a moment then suggested that his friend simply submit the incident report he had begun writing last night.  'Okay, that was a good start' thought Lloyd.  Then the always coordinated Bigglio chomped on his cigar and said, "I bet it will match up pretty well with the reports I had two of my people submit about her drunken behavior in the casino before I asked her to leave."

"You asked her to leave because she was drunk and disorderly?"  Lloyd asked feeling like there was a little ray of hope for his case.  Bigglio pulled the cigar from his mouth so his friend could get a clear view of his full devious grin then said, "As far as you know; and Webster too of course."

"Great!" responded Lloyd.  "May I see your memo?"

"Oh no" answered Giovanni with a magical wave of the hand.  "I didn't write a memo.  You know I don't like to get involved in these sorts of things.  But I did have two of my employees write reports of what they saw."

"May I see those?" he inquired hopefully.

"No, best not" explained Bigglio.  "You don't know about them yet."

Lloyd's vacant stare brought a better explanation from his friend.  "You just remain in the dark about whatever mysterious thing Webster was on about, and follow normal procedures by submitting that incident report you wrote last night.  I think that will lead to clearing things up for the simple minded Webster."

"Oh yeah, right" Canard said with a new, barely flickering light of understanding.  "I'd better go find that report I started."  As he rushed back towards his office on his newly refurbished hope-mobile, he quickly turned and said, "Thanks Giovanni, you're a life saver."

"What?" questioned Bigglio throwing his head back and his hands up into the air, "I didn't do nuthin!"

Whatever his methods Canard appreciated Bigglio's efforts and hoped he could repay him some time.  Gio wasn't really the type of person that ever seemed to be in need of anything or even to know what stress and worry were.  He was in a happy marriage with a great woman and loved his job.  If a man could make a living from playing games and watching others play games then he guessed it was all-in-all a pretty sweet deal.  He realized how much he envied Giovanni, but put it out of his mind fast.  He knew he could never do all the things Bigglio did and manage everything so seemingly effortlessly and always with such class and finesse.  Lloyd had a hero and it felt good to be around someone who seemed to have it all together.  There was no room for envy; Gio was a great friend.

On the way back to his office Canard became aware of the unusual silence and lack of personnel in the hallways.  It struck him as odd, but he was also very thankful for the respite.  Rounding the corner leading to the office he encountered a very odd and disturbing scene: a large German shepherd standing in his path.  The sight caused him to stop in his tracks.  Seconds later he realized the canine was on a lead being held by a person in a black helmet and dark blue jumpsuit with 'BOMB SQUAD' emblazoned across in large white letters.  That definitely wasn't a good sign.  The bomb dog stared at Canard with ears high in the air, but it was the helmeted man who barked, "Who are you?  What are you doing here?"

"I work here," Lloyd stumbled in confusion, "I'm the head of Bitewoody security, Lloyd Canard."

"Well Mr. Security Man, you should be the last one to breach a police line and enter a contaminated facility while the scene is still under assessment" the policeman reprimanded Canard ruthlessly.

"What's going on?" "I just came from the casino. Is this for real?"

The policeman gave him a hard look and reached for the microphone pinned to his shoulder, "I need an available unit to escort a civilian wandering around the premises," he transmitted.

"I am *not* a civilian" Lloyd said a bit too adamantly. His years in the military had engrained the belief that the title 'civilian' was a derogatory term.

"Okay Mr. Security Man from the casino," the policeman addressed him disrespectfully, "just wait where you are and we'll take care of you."

"But I don't need any help, I just want to know what's going on" he explained while taking two more steps in the direction of his office to exhibit his urgency.

"WAIT!" commanded the bomb squad officer as he let out some slack in the German shepherd's leash. To accentuate his point the officer squawked, "Heel Anouk!" to the tranquil dog. This was clearly more a threat to Canard than an actual instruction to the canine which had been trained for nothing beyond sniffing out explosives.

Lloyd was getting tired of being yelled at and given orders today. If he had wanted to be treated so rudely he could have simply stayed at home with Perla. Eyeing the dog that was uninterestingly eyeing him, he gave up trying to explain and remained where he was. He wondered how all this could have happened so quickly and without his having heard any alert or notification over the radio. Yet again Chief Canard found himself out of the loop; stabbed in the back by his officers and very publicly trapped on the outside of his own sphere of professional responsibility.

When another jump-suited officer arrived to escort Canard from the building Lloyd quietly complied and made neither protests nor inquiries. Once outside the complex he joined the other employees gathered in the parking lot. Police were interviewing a few people including a couple of his officers. Eager to learn what had happened, he moved in the direction of what appeared to be their operational command center. As he approached the officer scribbling on his clipboard Lloyd's ears were burning as he heard, "and that's when Chief Canard directed me to report the suspicious package and initiate emergency procedures."

Lloyd was incredibly surprised to hear his name being tossed about as if he had been intricately involved in managing this situation, but he was even more surprised to see that it was Officer Zambrano who was relaying this unexplained bit of information.

"What's going on?" he inquired, suspiciously concerned that his name was being included in police reports when he had no idea what was going on.

"Oh there you are Chief" piped up Zambrano with an air of helpfulness. "I was just telling the lieutenant how you initiated the emergency response."

"I initiated..." Lloyd began then stumbled for more words before finally asking, "the what?"

"Yes sir" recounted Zambrano. "Remember when you came out of Mr. Webster's office and told me there was a suspicious package outside the door?"

He focused all his attention on Zambrano as he tried to ignore the crowd of people around and the police lieutenant busily scribbling every word they spoke.

"Well Officer Zambrano," Lloyd began slowly, "I do remember making a remark to you about there being a hat hanging on the doorknob of Webster's office. But what could that possibly have to do with anything that is going on here?" Canard added this inquiry with a growing fear that the officer's response would confirm his sickening suspicion of what had transpired.

"Did you say a *hat*?" interjected the police lieutenant.

"Yes I did" answered Canard.

"You're not going to tell me this is all about a hat are you?" asked the obviously perturbed police officer as his head flitted back and forth between Zambrano and Canard in hopes of a clear answer.

"Oh no" he answered confidently. "I'm not the one who is going to explain this." Canard stared straight at Officer Zambrano and warned him, "You better have a good explanation of what happened after we saw the hat."

"Of course I do sir" responded Officer Zambrano with an arrogance that immediately caused Lloyd's chest to tighten in discomfort. Then he continued, "When you pointed out the beret to me you definitely used the adjective *suspicious* to emphasize your statement. Furthermore, to enhance the point you were obviously making, I quite distinctly recall your repeating the assertion with an exclamation intended to incite action on my part by employing the use of my professional title and name 'Officer Zambrano'".

Damn! Of all the knucklehead security officers he had working there Lloyd had to bump heads with the one that was working his way through law school.

"It was a hat" Canard pleaded with more emotion, yet much less eloquence than Zambrano's long-winded explanation.

But Zambrano wasn't yet through. "So it would seem Chief Canard, but as an officer under your charge and direction I had no reason to believe that your proposal was intentionally fraudulent with the purpose of maliciously misdirecting not only your own officer's professional efforts, but with the culmination of initiating waste, fraud and abuse of public safety personnel and resources."

He stared, silently fuming as this law student laid down the case against him.

Zambrano continued unabated by Canard's flaring nostrils, "So I responded in an appropriate manner, carrying forth with my duties as thoroughly trained and reacted in a manner fully intended to follow established emergency procedures and maximize the security and safety of all employees, customers, guests and stakeholders of the Bitewoody Executive Office Towers, Casino and Hotel."

Lloyd could see that Ned Zambrano was enjoying his little fifteen minutes of fame with an audience. He could also see very well that the police lieutenant taking notes seemed completely enthralled with Zambrano's response and very obviously considered Canard to be nothing more than an intruding idiot.

"It was nothing but a hat hanging on a doorknob!" Canard emphasized uselessly to the police lieutenant who could not even be bothered to give him a response. Canard's argument was wholly factual but lacked the fluency of Zambrano's legal prose, so he was yet again minimized and ignored. The annoyed cop rolled his eyes as he turned his back on Lloyd, lifted his handheld radio and began to call off the search. The police lieutenant then gave a polite nod and 'Thank you' to Zambrano, but didn't even acknowledge Canard as he ordered the bomb seeking officers to stand down.

Chief Canard instructed Zambrano, "Let everyone know the center has been cleared and employees may return to work."

"Yes sir" answered Zambrano.

As Lloyd turned to leave Zambrano asked, "Do you want me to write up the incident report?"

He didn't bother to turn around, but just lifted his arm to give a backhanded wave and said, "Don't worry about it; I'll take care of this one."

"Are you sure?" Zambrano tossed back.

Lloyd stopped in his tracks and turned around to face the insolent officer. He stared at officer Zambrano for a moment, observing the immature, cocky way he chewed his gum with excessive aggression. Finally he exploded with, "Just do what I've told you to do, and nothing more this time!" then turned to walk briskly back inside the building.

Back in his office Lloyd only took a few minutes to whip out a brief report of the previous evening's incident with the cashier. He even went so far as to include the heart-warming part about asking one of his officers to walk her to a cab. The truth was that he told the officer to follow her drunk ass outside to the taxi queue and make sure she didn't try to drive in her condition. He didn't care so much for the welfare of the cashier as he did about avoiding an even greater amount of paperwork that would be generated by her having an accident on the premises. Not to mention the way Lady Luck's evil twin sister flashed her snaggle-toothed smile in his direction, it would almost certainly be his car that the intoxicated woman would crash into. But creative writing can be an effective weapon so Lloyd employed it to his benefit on this occasion. And why not? That wicked alcoholic cashier had certainly interpreted the previous evening's event in a much different and horrendously vicious manner. It was too bad he didn't have his favorite buffer Brittle around last night. He'd have to find a way to discreetly put Brittle on that cashier's trail once this incident died down. That would fix her. Though Brittle was a difficult man to supervise, his irritatingly unstoppable persistence could be a very useful tool in the game of revenge. Like a blindfolded rhinoceros in a crystal factory, once you gave him a slap to get started Brittle would run rampant, full-force and destroy whatever was in his path.  If he could just guide Russell in the right direction the man might actually be of some use in getting back at that obnoxious, lying, alcoholic cashier.

Though the morning's excitement left the building empty at the regular 8:15 AM meeting time, Mr. Bitewoody was determined to have his private audience and insisted that everyone convene in his office at 11:30 AM.  The CEO obviously had no concern about anyone else's work obligations or desires to take a lunch break.  Lloyd Canard hated being the center of attention, but no matter how hard he tried to blend in and not be seen something beyond his control always seemed to push him back into the spotlight.  Recent events had conspired to create all sorts of new scuttlebutt and jokes directed at Canard.

There was the little comment about, "If you can't beat your own wife, then find someone else to whip on at work."

Proof that Markey failed to keep his word was revealed when someone else made the snickering comment, "If you ain't getting what you need at home just bring an extra t-shirt to the office."

Although these quips were really not funny at all, most everyone laughed at the jokes except Lloyd.  They really didn't have to be humorous since their only true intention was to focus constant negative attention on Bitewoody's favorite whipping boy Chief Canard.  Vice President Webster was too much of a brown-nosing wimp to rebuff the comments or defend him so Lloyd was on his own.  While Canard never enjoyed the 8:15 AM meeting, todays was notably one of the worst.  Through this useless forum, the Chief learned that the rumor mill had somehow morphed several stories together to create the completely bogus tale that Canard had beaten up the mother who had given birth in the casino when she walked into his office and caught the final throes of his solo act.  It mattered little that the three incidents occurred on different days and that the story was ridiculously far-fetched.  To those who feasted on rumors, fueling their growth and aiding their dissemination, the more absurd the story the more quickly it was passed along.  Lloyd imagined that tomorrow's version of the fictitious tale would probably have the poor woman's newborn infant exiting the womb wearing a beret.

When Lloyd was called for the second time today with instructions to report to Mr. Webster's office he was quite perturbed. What kind of crap was this cashier stirring up now and why was Webster too much of an idiot to realize that this was a huge waste of time. Canard was surprised when Webster invited him in with an uncommon smile and eagerly offered him a chair. Webster stood and paced around the room with what appeared to be excitement. Lloyd hoped that the cashier had been fired. No such luck there.

Webster revealed his newfound pride in what he described as, "A bold new vision to streamline the functionasity of our agency."

Lloyd was not positive, but felt quite sure that 'functionasity' wasn't even an actual word. Mr. Webster was a college graduate and business major so he was prone to spin long, nonsensical words into indecipherable phrases like this that really communicated nothing and revealed not an ounce of information about what it was supposed to mean. It was Canard's experience that college business students were instructed to develop these so-called visionary statements as they were both important sounding as well as sufficiently vague enough that they could not be held responsible for any undesirable results later on. In the business community it was rare that anything be challenged anyway as to do so required one to admit a failure to comprehend. So whenever these types ran up against an inconceivable visionary statement or business proposal their usual reaction was to jump up and give a standing ovation so they could be seen by both peers and superiors as being knowledgeable and 'on board' with the newest groundbreaking proposition. Much like politics and magic tricks, the corporate world too was built upon elaborate distractions and fantastic fabrications.

Lloyd snapped out of his daydream as he heard Webster announce, "That's where you come in."

"Sir?" he asked blankly. He had drifted away and missed the last minute or so of Webster's normally superfluous rant.

"I want you to put it together" Webster explained.

Not wanting to admit that he hadn't bothered to listen to his bosses instructions Lloyd tried, "Okay sir. Will you email me the basic outline you envision for where this project will lead?"

"What outline Canard?" Webster said as if disappointed at his subordinate's inability to grasp such a simple concept. "Simply put together a policy which clearly delineates and explains the new organizational restriction on communications between employees on different levels of the organizational hierarchy."

Lloyd tried not to let his expression show his confusion as he asked, "So you want me to write a new standard operating procedure which alters the way we communicate within the organization?"

"Yes, that's correct" confirmed Webster.

"And this policy will prohibit communication between employees of different ranks and functions?" he asked, now totally confused.

"Exactly" Webster said excitedly as he felt Canard finally seemed to understand.

"So," Lloyd continued, "should we call this a new 'closed door' policy?"

"No. No we can't say that," the V.P. answered quickly, "but we can say that it's a new chain of command policy."

He now had a better picture of what his boss wanted...and while he knew it was an idiotic plan he also knew he couldn't come out and bluntly tell him so. Instead Canard attempted to ask questions that would hopefully jog Webster's underemployed brain towards a better understanding of just how stupid his suggestion sounded.

"Okay. Once I've written this policy what should I do with it?" he inquired tactfully.

"Bring it to me for approval," Webster answered simply.

"But wouldn't that put me and you in violation of the new policy?" Canard asked.

"What?" Webster inquired, unclear of his meaning.

"What I mean sir," he attempted to explain in a polite, manner since he was basically revealing his boss as an idiot, "is that by the new chain of command policy, you and I will not be allowed to communicate."

"That is unless you intend to promote me right away." He added this joke as an unplanned afterthought.

Webster either missed Canard's poor attempt at humor or intentionally ignored it to avoid discussing the promotion reference. The V.P. looked stumped for a moment then a flash of brilliance crossed his face as he explained, "Oh no, that won't be a problem. The policy will not actually be effective until I sign it so we'll be covered."

Mr. Webster did not yet comprehend the real issue here so Lloyd tried again with as much tact as possible when handling an incompetent boss, "Okay sir, and once the policy has been signed what would you have me do with it?"

He looked at the Chief as if just noticing his ignorance for the very first time, "Of course, Mr. Canard, you will introduce and explain the policy to all of your employees."

"But how could I do that sir?" Lloyd asked imitating genuine concern. "I'd be in violation of communicating with employees on a level other than my own." This time he deliberately refrained from including a comment suggesting demotion.

"Oh, but that would be different," was Webster's unclear and obviously uncertain response.

Lloyd now felt that he was getting through so he persisted, "And I'd be unable to attend the 8:15 AM meetings any longer because it would require communication across forbidden hierarchal barriers. And I'd be restricted from passing along instructions to subordinates as well as denied the possibility of sharing important information with you and upper management." He finished and felt triumphant as he saw the look of distraught understanding flow across Webster's furrowed brow. Lloyd tried hard to exhibit only a look of professional concern on his own face.

"Aaahh, well maybe you and I should both make some notes on this issue and reconvene later for further discussion," Webster suggested.

Lloyd thought that was a pretty good save for his boss and was much more comfortable that this ludicrous conversation ended that way. Of course, he had no serious intention of making any notes and knew that he'd never put his name on any policy of that kind. If this ridiculous subject ever came up for discussion again it certainly wouldn't be his doing.

As Canard was departing his boss's office, Webster added as an afterthought, "Oh, and by the way, try to find a way to curtail your officers from accosting me in the hallway with questions; you know I'm very busy."

"Yes sir," was Lloyd's final comment on his way out the door.

'Aha!' So that was it; now he understood what had caused this confusing waste of time concerning some idiotic 'chain of command policy.' All this mess resulted from one of Canard's overzealous employees approaching Steve Webster in the hallway with a work related question which the V.P. was evidently unable to answer. So, rather than brushing up on policy and providing the officer with the answer, he felt it would be a more appropriate response to simply outlaw interoffice communications completely. Sadly, this was a typical response from upper management.

Lloyd somehow managed to elude the bad luck gremlins for the remainder of the workday and decided to pop into the casino bar for a quick drink before heading home. Here he found a bit of comfort as he was somewhat able to sink into anonymity as the evening crowd came into the bar for happy hour. Once sufficiently lubricated from half price liquor, the crowd inevitably moved into the casino and willingly fed their hard-earned money into the pockets of Lancaster Bitewoody. The smoky room echoed sounds of rolling dice and slapping chips alongside the laughs of winners and the groans of losers. The brightly flashing machines and short-skirted waitresses serving up even more alcohol created the perfect atmosphere to extract the dollars and common sense from these silly people. What a great scam Lloyd thought. Too bad he was only a lower-level employee whose only benefit was reduced price drinks. Well, the least he could do was restrict his activity to the bar where he could suck down reduced price drinks and forgo the overpayment through eventual losses in the casino. Canard didn't go for casinos and gambling. His haphazard life was devoid of anything resembling luck and he was too accustomed with the failures of everyday life to ever submit to a game of chance. In Lloyd's case it might as well be a game of no chance so he didn't even bother to try. Besides, he felt more and more like a winner every time he finished another watered down employee discounted drink saving 65 cents.

Giovanni Bigglio found his friend sitting in the corner and stopped by briefly. He was the only person Lloyd could trust to share the story of that stupid new policy idea he'd been pitched earlier by Mr. Webster. Bigglio chuckled at the story and said, "That's our Webster," as he shook his head in disapproval. Casino business called Giovanni away after only a couple minutes and Lloyd figured that was a good cue for his own departure.

The thought of Perla simultaneously bewildered and frustrated him.  She made a fuss if he arrived home late, but never made a meal or anything else that he was actually late for.  Of course it was also true that she found something to argue about every day regardless of what time he made it home from work.  He assumed it was probably only because she wished to ensure that he received his daily dosage of nagging as prescribed by Doctor Perla herself.  On that note, there was yet another annoying habit of his wife that bothered Lloyd to no end.  For some unexplained reason she insisted on viewing the poo of every family member.  She actually imagined that she could diagnose all sorts of things through poo review.  Maybe even predict the future or reveal secrets of the past.  Evidently she fancied herself some sort of medical doctor or diviner.  He considered the term 'witch doctor' to be a much more appropriate title for his wife, but like so many of the things going on in his mind he kept that thought to himself as well.  Lloyd could not imagine what it was she found so fascinating about human waste, but as long as the neighbors didn't find out and she restricted the perverse diversion to include only the family stools, Lloyd decided that though it was thoroughly weird, it was probably mostly harmless.  It was oddly inexplicable and Lloyd assumed that it was simply part of her master plan to drive him towards an early death through frequent injections of unnecessary stress.  Of course, Lloyd's habit of treating the stress with massive inoculations of Scotch combined with the lack of a proper diet were probably just as bad for his overall health.

Lloyd entered their home to find Perla in the living room with several large shopping bags.  She had clothing laid out across the coffee table and the sofa as she was apparently admiring her recent acquisitions.  He didn't have to speak a word as the look on his face alone communicated clearly what was on his mind.

"Don worry," consoled Perla.  "Everyting wuz on sale."

"Oh well then, I guess if it was on sale then you just *had* to buy it" responded Lloyd sarcastically.

"Dats right" answered Perla totally missing the sarcasm.  She began quoting price comparisons and summed it all up with the proud declaration, "Wid all the sales I saved over $400!"

She then crossed her arms in triumph as she dared her husband to find fault in that.  The fact that she had purchased six hundred dollars worth of decorations, flatware, candle holders, picture frames, hats, lamps and of course shoes that they neither needed nor would likely ever use totally escaped her extremely limited insight. He closed his eyes in disbelief at her blatant economic ignorance, then turned to walk away while saying, "That's just great Perla. Now go deposit that $400 you saved in the bank!"

In the evening he sat down with his daughter Andi to discuss her less than stellar performance in school. He attempted to counsel the teenager about how getting better grades would improve her chances for college as well as expand the possibility of future opportunities in school as well as throughout her life. He tried to stress to her that each step, no matter how small, is an important building block in constructing a successful career and comfortable life. That's when Perla walked in, overheard her husband's comments and couldn't resist inserting her own unsolicited two cents worth.

"She can always get a yob at McDonalds," Perla volunteered.

Lloyd felt his jaw muscles clench reflexively then continued, "Yes, that's true Andi, you can work part time to assist with college tuition, books and other educational expenses, to have pocket money and eventually buy yourself a car."

Perla chimed in again, "Don tell her she hav to go to university. She kin jus as well work at McDonalds if she wan to!"

Lloyd tried to remain calm. For his daughter's sake he wanted to get this critical point across.

"Sure, you can work at McDonalds if you have to, but that is not the type of thing that people usually aim for."

"She hav to mek her own decision" Perla blurted defensively.

He had no idea what his wife could possibly be defending except for the fact that she continually felt compelled to contradict him, put him down, disregard his advice and ultimately belittle his mere existence.

"Andi will make her own decisions when she is grown, but it is up to us now as parents to guide her in the right direction" Lloyd responded with as much calm as he could muster under these circumstances. He attempted to regain control of the situation by explaining to them both, "A teenager, young adult if you will, must *learn* the art of decision making. Every emotional impulse cannot be acted upon without thoughtful consideration of consequences. That is the challenge of making the transition from adolescence to adulthood."

"Well you kin say all dat," Perla declared, "but she will have to mek di choice."

"Exactly" he retorted, reversing psychology by pretending to appreciate her assistance in proving his point. "If she doesn't do better in school she will not have any decisions to make because she will have no options in life."

"Options are always positive things." He took a slightly different direction now to explain his point, "One never wants to feel trapped by circumstance. There isn't much worse in life than being in a position you despise, but not having the ability to make a move and create an alternate opportunity to improve your overall situation."

"In fact, options are a very valuable thing in every aspect of your life." Lloyd continued now rather more introspectively, "Without them you will suffer from discomfort, disappointment and extreme difficulty in finding successful methods of dealing with the inevitable pains and challenges you must traverse in life."

Perla exhaled loudly with a, "Herumph!" to proclaim her doubt.

His point made most of his poise lost; Lloyd excused himself from the room without another word. His impromptu speech to his overly distracted daughter was meant to be a motivator to help guide her on the right track to a prosperous, happy and successful life. Then when Perla saw a chance to strike so she jumped in and, as usual, made a mockery of his advice. What had began as a pep talk for his teenager had resulted in a sad review of his own miserable failures in life. Canard had been a poor student, barely graduating high school and running off to the Marine Corps because he thought that would mean he'd never have to go to school again. Lloyd had traveled a long, bumpy road these past twenty-five years. He still regretted not having made better decisions about school and he still suffered the pains from a few other major life choices he'd selected. Lloyd felt trapped at home and trapped at work. His only space between the two was his commute, and he hated dealing with South Florida drivers who obviously held no concern for either their own safety or that of others on the road. They were almost all angry, rude, extremely self-centered and clearly enjoyed exhibiting their suicidal tendencies nearly as much as showing off their ability to honk the horn while raising one finger high in the air.

Lloyd went to bed that night with the dubitable sense that he'd failed to inspire his daughter and moreover feeling quite deflated himself. How did he expect to dole out honest, useful advice when it seemed that he had never himself heeded similar guidance? Lloyd guessed that this realization was yet another sign of aging when you are haunted by the déjà vu memory of hearing your parents' words reverberating out of your own mouth.

# *** DAY THREE ***

# Wednesday

In the morning, Lloyd's first stop in the office was by the main entrance security station known as Post One. Here he could review log books and any reports generated overnight. This would hopefully prepare him for dealing with the shift supervisor, and eventually the meeting with Mr. Bitewoody. Post One was the primary nerve center for the B.E.O.T.C.H. security operation at all times and the principle stationary post during the night shift. What caught his eye first this morning was a sign that evidently was meant to be amusing. Someone had placed a notice on the window reporting a lost hat; complete with a color photo of a black beret cut out of a catalog. He didn't bother to ask who had put it there as he knew he'd never get a straight answer from the officer on duty. Lloyd wasn't in the mood to even discuss the ridiculous incident any further so he simply ripped the poster down without comment or eye contact with the officer on Post One. He started to throw it in the trash can then thought better of that move and instead shoved the crumpled paper into his pocket to prevent its resurrection. He was in a pretty good mood this morning so he made a conscious decision not to let the juvenile pranks of his impudent officers bother him this time.

Today being Secretary's Day, Lloyd came prepared with a surprise for Miss Jordan. Apart from being quite nice to look at, she wasn't really much use. He did have to admit that Liz was very skilled in answering the telephone, but that was probably the result of most incoming calls being for her. For whatever reason, Miss Jordan insisted on calling herself his 'administrative assistant' rather than secretary. He supposed her choice of term might actually look better on a résumé.

Chief Canard probably put more time into selecting Liz's gift than the average boss, but he was quite happy with his ultimate selection. The surprise was a very beautiful flowering plant in a vase. In the base of the pot, where you would normally find soil, this particular plant had none. This was a special plant, with only water surrounding the exposed roots along with a very colorful exotic fish. This flowering plant and puffy-cheeked fish created their own mini eco-system. As it was explained to him, you never had to feed either: the fish would feed on the roots of the plant and the plant would feed on the natural fertilizer produced by the fish. It all seemed really unique and quite simple to maintain. Lloyd came into work early and left the fish bowl wrapped in a fancy red bow along with a card in Liz's office to surprise her.

When he was returning from morning rounds he encountered Miss Jordan in the hallway. The look on Liz's face was something other than surprise but he proceeded with the greeting, "Happy Secre..., uh, I mean Administrative Assistant's Day. Sorry about that, but, uhm, happy day nonetheless."

"Thank you," Liz responded, "and like, thanks for the card and the flower."

Lloyd smiled proudly, but Miss Jordan had more to say.

"Actually, Mr. Canard," Liz continued hesitantly as she bit her lower lip in a way that unnecessarily excited her boss, "I have come to like, register a protest."

"Huh?" he responded in confusion. "What do you mean?"

"I mean," persisted Elizabeth, "that I do not think it is like, proper to imprison another being and treat it as some form of like, property."

He could tell she was in a weird mood and knew this wasn't going be any fun at all. He placed his hands together in front of his waist as he contemplated what she could mean before asking, "Miss Jordan, you have me at a great disadvantage here. I really don't know what in the world has happened to upset you. I think you may be indicating that you view your employment here as being equivalent to some form of incarceration. I honestly do not believe that I have ever treated you in a manner that could possibly be described in so dastardly a way. I have to ask that you please explain."

"Mr. Canard, obviously it's like, about this Secretaries Day business and the horrible thing I found on my desk with your name on it" Liz shrieked quite distraught.

He noticed right away that she'd said 'secretary' rather than 'administrative assistant' this time, but decided not to mention it since she was already distraught. He was more concerned with her claim that he had left something horrible on her desk.

So he inquired, "Are you referring to the gift?" in what he hoped was a calm and sincere tone.

"It's like, an abomination to God!" she answered excitedly, now with tears welling in her eyes.

At this point Lloyd was sure that someone, probably one of his officers who'd been previously rebuffed by the fair Liz, must have vandalized the gift. Canard stood and told Liz, "I'm sorry this has you so upset. I'll go remove it right now."

On the way he wondered what bizarre scene he would discover upon arrival. Most certainly the fish had been killed. Maybe the corpse was splayed across her keyboard, or skewered with the letter opener on the bulletin board or stapled savagely to the back of her chair. Whatever it was, damn it, he'd love to get his hands on the culprit.

When he arrived at the office he very chivalrously asked Liz to wait outside the door until he cleaned things up. She thanked him through sobs as this seemed to prod her into releasing pent up emotions. He entered Miss Jordan's office warily; not wanting to disturb any possible evidence as well as concerned with what monstrous scene he might find. He scanned the room, her desk, chair and keyboard for any traces of the dead and disemboweled fish. He saw nothing out of place. He looked at the fish bowl on top of the file cabinet where he had left it and saw the bug-eyed, fat-cheeked little red fish staring back at him. The pot didn't appear to have been disturbed at all. It even had the ribbon still wrapped around it. He was confused, but looked carefully around once again to be sure that he had not missed something. Finally giving up, Lloyd called, "Miss Jordan, can you come in here please?"

Liz entered the room with one hand covering her mouth and the other on top of her eyes with just the tiniest crack open for peeking out. "Is it gone yet?" she asked hopefully.

"Yes it appears to be all clear now" he answered reassuringly. "Can you tell me what it was that...?"

"AAAAYYYYY!!" Lloyd jumped in surprise as his question was both interrupted and made moot in the same instant. Liz's unexpected wail of terror sounded something akin to a hoarse banshee snagging a hangnail on an Alpaca sweater.

"It's still there!" she added to her scream.

"But where?" asked Lloyd glancing around for the hidden demon which taunted her.

"Right there like, on top of the cabinet!" she said in a tone which portrayed her agony in even acknowledging its existence.

"But..." Canard stammered, "do you mean the fishbowl I gave you as a gift?"

"Yes of course" Liz answered with her trembling hands still covering her eyes. "It's absolutely horrid!"

"Horrid?" questioned Lloyd with the feeling that she was being a bit too dramatic for the occasion. And thanks to his wife Perla's astute study and frequent portrayal of poor soap opera acting he was truly capable of recognizing extreme overreacting. If Liz didn't want a gift or simply didn't like the gift he'd chosen, she surely could have said something or just have given it away. He was aware of how much many young women loved drama, but this incredible scene she was creating seemed very immature and totally unnecessary in Lloyd's insignificant opinion.

She attempted to explain, "I'm sorry, but I just like, don't think it's right for me to accept the gift of life from you Mr. Canard."

"The gift of life?" Lloyd repeated warily in question form. Then added "What?"

"I think the best thing for like, everyone is to set him free," she suggested.

He was very uncomfortable with this odd turn of events and the fact that she now appeared to be advocating for the fish's freedom. Miss Jordan's ridiculous antics led him to believe that it would probably be best to remove the gift immediately and to never mention it again. Without another word and while intentionally avoiding eye contact, he retrieved the fishbowl and walked past Liz who still had her eyes partially covered. He quickly carried the vase and contents into his own office where it would remain out of sight and hopefully soon be forgotten. Canard then closed his office door, had a seat and began a review of messages and recent activity reports in preparation for the dreaded meeting about nothing. He was pretty sure the story of his horribly backfiring gift would feed the rampant Bitewoody rumor mill. It was too bad that the same exchange of positive information and policies didn't occur among staff. Oh no, they couldn't remember policy, procedures or instructions, but any rumor was immediately given top priority in their feeble memory cells. He couldn't remember how many times his officer's had used the juvenile excuse 'I didn't know' in response to some error or omission they made in the dismal performance of their duties; yet they never seemed at a loss for the massive amount of data, or rather dirt, associated with the numerous rumors making the rounds of the massive B.E.O.T.C.H. Rumor fueled innuendo was always passed along without fail while useful, relevant data was ignored and inevitably allowed to fall between the cracks.

On the way to the morning meeting Canard made a pass by the supervisor's office to ensure there had been no kids born during the night and was happy to hear the answer was a negative. Of course, that's the same thing he had been told last time so he wasn't very trusting of the information his officers passed along. There wasn't enough time to see Bigglio before the meeting so he just shrugged his shoulders, crossed his fingers and hoped for the best.

As had become commonplace the last several weeks, the meeting began with CEO Bitewoody giving updates on his displeasure with the contractors building his new Olympic size, in-ground swimming pool. The fingers of Mr. Bitewoody's left hand twiddled with the tip of his heavily waxed, mayonnaise colored mustache as he delivered his tale of woe. The man didn't seem to realize that his subordinates were not his peers, and therefore were not able to conceptualize the same misery he suffered from such excessive wealth. Most of these people couldn't even afford to live in a subdivision with a community pool, let alone ever achieve ownership of a home with enough surrounding land to dig a hole of sufficient measurement to accommodate more than a mere soaking of their tired feet. But Bitewoody was of a different world and had never had to struggle with living on the precipice of poverty. In fact, like many of the ultra-rich, he was completely ignorant that such a state even existed.

It's not that the morning meeting was originally designed to be so completely without agenda or purpose, but it had evolved into something more like a club meeting in the lounge where any subject could be brought up and endlessly dwelt upon without relevance to anyone's actual job. Canard sat quietly as he felt himself tense uncontrollably at the urge to rip his own hair out in frustration. Others in the meeting feigned interest or even asked questions to prolong the ridiculous conversation. He assumed that these people either found some twisted pleasure from this meaningless meeting or actually had no real work to accomplish. Of course the meeting would have been incomplete without someone bringing up the previous day's bomb threat confusion. He was still annoyed by that mess and professionally embarrassed that he had so little control over what his officers got up to. Once the subject of the beret had been broached it was almost on cue that Mr. Bitewoody reached under the table, pulled something out of a paper bag and tossed the burgundy beret on the table. Snickers and giggles rippled around the conference table.

"Suspicious ain't it?" quipped Bitewoody and the room erupted with rude, unconstrained laughter from the crowd of brown-nosers surrounding him. The truth was that Chief Canard supervised the largest department at the Bitewoody complex and the only one that operated fully staffed, continually; twenty-four hours a day, every single day of the year. Additional truths were that his workforce had the least education, least training, lowest budget, highest turnover rate and not surprisingly the most problems. Considering all of these undeniable challenges the other department heads didn't envy the security chief's position one bit, but they sure did get a kick out of making jokes and pointing out deficiencies. Oh yeah, they were full of criticism and useless comments, but not one of them was ever able to offer any critical input or valid suggestions. Canard had spent his entire career in the fields of security and law enforcement so he was well aware of the tendency of the protected to belittle, ignore and minimize security procedures and personnel until the time something really hit the fan. On days like these Lloyd often fantasized that something bad really would happen to get these people's attention. It would be even better if the trouble were to kick off at exactly 8:15 AM!

After the final release from that tortuous meeting, Lloyd headed for his office with hope of getting some actual work done. As he was passing near the lobby he overheard shouting. He immediately went to see what was going on. He found one of the vice presidents of the Union Bank and Trust exchanging words rather loudly with the officer in Post One.

Post One was a state-of-the-art security control center. It was constructed of reinforced steel walls, floor and ceiling with impenetrable ballistic glass windows. From this secure box a solitary security officer could control entry and exit points, monitor elevator operations and view the dozens of security cameras throughout the Bitewoody Business Tower and surrounding perimeter. The officer assigned to this post was responsible for confirming that only authorized personnel were allowed access beyond the common areas and ensuring any visitors to more sensitive areas were positively identified, documented and escorted. While this structure was admirably quite safe from breach, it was also overly soundproof and communication between the officer inside and people on the outside was an extremely difficult task. For the most part employees entering the center simply showed their identification badges, sometimes followed by a polite wave and less commonly accompanied by a friendly smile. The rarity of such a smile combined with the utterly soundproof box tended to have an awkwardly negative effect on the employee inside. Officers who worked Post One on a regular basis tended to grow increasingly more paranoid as they assumed that the people outside the box were somehow taunting or talking about them. The angry and confusing responses exhibited by the officer on display in the glass box eventually taught the few grinning offenders that a grimace was not only more appropriate but somehow oddly much more appreciated. It was specifically that extraordinary sound-proofing which contributed to the problem on this particular Wednesday morning. Chief Canard placed himself between the two men arguing through the small paper slot and instructed them both to calm down and be quiet. He then asked Mr. Gorham to have a seat in the lobby and promised to assist him personally. The angry bank manager grumbled and gave another rude look to the officer, but did comply and take a seat along with his confused guest. Lloyd entered Post One and asked the Security Officer, Duane Victorin, to explain what was going on.

"I don't know what happened Chief" Victorin answered. "I saw Mr. Gorham crossing the lobby with that other gentleman and I just reminded him that the man would need a guest pass."

"Is that all?" Lloyd asked rather suspiciously, as his experience taught him that his officers were most often the instigators of these problems.

"Yes sir Chief" the officer confirmed. "And then he marched up to my window and began questioning me about why it was necessary."

"Really?" asked Lloyd thoughtfully "I've never had any problems like this from Mr. Gorham."

"Then he told me that he had never heard of that policy before," Officer Victorin further explained, "I guess that person with him must be some big wig he wants to impress, because he started shouting at me like he had some kind of authority to ignore security and make his own rules."

"That does sound strange" agreed the chief. "Let me speak to him and see if he acts like that with me."

"He called me a doorman-in-a-box" the officer added with anguish in his voice.

"Yeah, well you know your job is much more than that Duane" confirmed Canard with a slap of support on the young man's shoulder. "Don't let one man's ignorance and unprofessionalism get you down."

He left Post One to hear Mr. Gorham's side of the story. The brief timeout hadn't provided the calming affect Canard had hoped for. The bank manager sprung from his chair and immediately released a tirade of bottled accusations, "You have to get control of your people Chief! Sometimes they seem to be hell bent on hampering productivity. You should know, some of us have *real* work to do and your officers are only getting in the way of much more important matters than they are even capable of comprehending!"

Lloyd put on a large smile and said, "Thank you for that robust assessment Mr. Gorham." This was a very useful tactic which he enjoyed using on irate people who exhibited a confidence in their superiority and a strong urge to argue. A smiling, courteous response was exactly what they didn't want to see when they were itching for a fight. It was an extremely successful disarming tactic that never failed to knock them down a peg and show them who was really in control.

"Now," Canard began in a calm voice to display his dominance, "if you would be so kind as to relay to me what happened I am sure that it can all be sorted out most expediently."

Mr. Gorham blinked a couple times as he attempted to adjust to the surprising way the Chief had humbled him. He was noticeably uncomfortable to begin with, but then settled down and said, "Well Chief, when I uhm, came in with my associate your officer stopped us and told me that we could not proceed to my office."

"Is that all he told you?" Lloyd inquired.

"No, actually it wasn't" Mr. Gorham explained. "He told us that we could only enter the building if my associate donned a gas mask."

Lloyd paused a moment to figure out what sense this made. Since it didn't make any at all, he asked for clarification. "Did you say *gas mask*?"

"Yes I did" confirmed the Union Bank Vice President. "The officer actually instructed us that gas masks were required by policy."

"Well," Lloyd said feeling a little less control now, "I agree with you about that being odd." Then he inquired, "Did the officer provide any explanation?"

"The only response I could get out of him was that it was a long-standing security policy. I told him I'd never heard anything so ridiculous, but he absolutely insisted," explained Mr. Gorham.

"That is a new one on me as well" Lloyd attempted to joke as he was feeling less confident with this new information. "Let me find out what's going on."

Canard returned to Officer Victorin in Post One and asked, "Did you say anything to Mr. Gorham about having to wear a gas mask?"

"What?!" squawked the officer excitedly, "of course I didn't say that!" "All I told him was that his visitor required a guest pass and then he just went flipping crazy on me!" the frustrated officer finished.

"Hold on a minute" said Lloyd as the wheels in his mind slowly turned in a new direction. "Did you tell him that he needed a *guest pass?*" questioned Lloyd.

"Yes sir, Chief" responded the officer. "That's what I've been saying the whole time."

"It's okay Duane, I believe you" consoled Canard. "I think this mess was just an inadvertent misunderstanding."

Lloyd asked Mr. Gorham to come over to Post One. Standing in the open doorway between them the Chief explained to them both, "I'm pretty sure what happened was the fault of this mostly sound proof room. When Officer Victorin reminded you that your visitor needed a 'guest pass' you mistakenly thought he said 'gas mask.' Then when you, Mr. Gorham, challenged the odd request, Officer Victorin assumed that you were balking at routine security procedures."

The adversaries eyed each other speculatively and then slowly eased their tense stares as they realized the error. Mr. Gorham offered an embarrassed apology and hand shake to Officer Victorin and the air was clear. Lloyd waited for a moment more while the officer issued a visitor badge to the bank manager's guest and then walked towards his own office.

It was simply amazing how ridiculous things could get sometimes. It's almost as if everyone was purposely going out of their way to try to create problems. Here you had a workplace made up of many different people performing a variety of functions with the sole purpose of accomplishing the singular goal of success for B.E.O.T.C.H. Yet anytime you threw together so many people, there inevitably arose a sense of competition and struggle for territory, which always seemed to end in a mess of confusion and havoc.

Security Supervisor Nick Swath popped out of an adjacent hallway just as he was passing by. Lloyd was certain that this man was as good at stalking him as he was at eluding work.

"Hey boss," Nick began as usual, "I hope you're doing alright today." Then he plowed on into his real reason for appearing out of the shadows, "Man, I think that guy set you up yesterday."

"What guy?"

"You know, that bookworm Zambulio," Swath answered.

"You mean Zambrano?" questioned Lloyd.

"Yeah, yeah. That's the one. He thinks he's so smart because he goes to college. Maaan, I tell you boss, I seen a whole lot more fools come out of college than ever went into college."

Lloyd had doubts about Nick's unusual statistics, but he knew that the man was just trying to make a connection with him. It was no secret that Canard had received his education in the Corps rather than on some lush campus. Not in the mood for his offensive antics at the moment, Lloyd asked, "Let's just keep this between us for now and see if that mess will blow over."

"Oh yeah boss" Swath responded with a conspiratorial glace down the empty hallway. "I'll just keep my eyes and ears open for any information you might find useful."

Lloyd gave him a surreptitious thumbs up, and Swath tiptoed away as he returned to his patented ultra-low profile.

With all the drama and distractions so far today, he hoped to finally find a little quiet back in his office. He was fairly certain that Liz wouldn't be bothering him with unnecessary conversation after that demoralizing gift fiasco. But peace and solitude were hard things to find and Lloyd seemed to be almost constantly stalked by trouble, idiots, troubled idiots, idiots in trouble, troublesome idiots and of course, idiots with the unique desire to introduce trouble where it did not yet exist.

As soon as he arrived at the entrance to his office Lloyd realized what a hopelessly stupid idea hiding in his own office was; of course anyone looking for him would start there. And who he saw roaming the hallway like a hungry, circling shark made it even worse. Waiting for him was Ernie Sauter, the lead representative for the security officer's union.

Lloyd braced himself for another attack of the ridiculous as he poorly faked a smile and reached out to shake Sauter's cool, limp hand.

"What can I do for you Mr. Sauter?"

"Good morning Chief," Sauter began politely, "I'm here on union business. May we talk in your office?"

Lloyd hated to let the guy get comfortable, but saw no way around it as he responded, "Sure, come on in."

Canard took his seat behind the desk and Sauter sat down uninvited, looking way too relaxed already.

"What can I do for you today?" he inquired politely while trying to hide his apprehension. A call from the union steward was never an indication of things going well.

"Well we have some serious concerns about an unfair management practice that has been ongoing for a while" Sauter began.

"Is this a problem we've discussed previously?" Lloyd asked for clarification.

"No sir. This is an issue which we've never addressed, but has been regularly occurring for almost two weeks now."

"Okay," Lloyd said expecting the worst, "tell me about it Mr. Sauter."

"Well Chief, the day shift supervisor has been using a bad clock to begin the shift for the past two weeks or so," he explained.

"What do you mean by 'a bad clock'?" Canard questioned.

"The clock in the supervisor's office is five minutes ahead of the actual time," Sauter detailed, "and the supervisor has been documenting officers coming to work late because he is using the wrong time."

"So what is your proposed solution?" Canard asked politely.

"Sir, we want the clock corrected, the officers exonerated and we additionally believe it would be appropriate for the supervisor to issue an apology," Sauter detailed in a practiced, overzealous manner of always negotiating for more than he expected was actually achievable.

"Well, first let me tell you what I would do in your situation." Lloyd proceeded slowly, "if my place of employment used a clock whose time didn't match mine then I would simply synchronize my watch to match it."

"I see what you're saying sir," responded the union representative without actually pausing to consider the advice, "but the fact is that the duty clock is wrong."

"How many officers have been written up for being late because of this confusion?" Canard asked diplomatically.

"Four sir," Sauter answered quickly.

"Is that four today or four total?" Canard narrowed his focus in on the real issue.

"Well, it's the same four officers who have been written up several times in the past two weeks," Sauter told him.

"Are their similar complaints coming from officers on the other two shifts?"

Sauter hesitated briefly as he hadn't anticipated this question, "No Chief, not yet. But I'm sure they'll be coming."

"Okay, let me see if I understand this correctly." Canard paused for effect then summarized: "The clock in the supervisor's office is off by five minutes which has caused the same four officers out of nearly three dozen on the day shift to be five minutes late several times over the past two weeks or so that you estimate this problem has been going on."

"Yes sir, that's it," Sauter said with the hope of a quick victory in his voice.

Lloyd sensed it and placed his hand over his mouth to cover his near smile with a more appropriately pensive look.

"I tell you what I'll do Mr. Sauter. I'll talk with the supervisor and look at the clock, but I want to be sure that I'm being fair to all parties."

"What do you mean sir?" the steward asked a bit unsure of where this was leading.

"Before I make a move on this I want you to bring me the time cards of these four employees so I can be sure that they have been staying an extra five minutes at the end of their shift to ensure that they are actually working the full eight hours they have been claiming" Canard detailed.

He could see the lump quiver in Sauter's throat as he pondered how to proceed. Then Canard helped him by offering an easy out, "I'm not going to take any action until you can fill me in on that last remaining data. So at your convenience Mr. Sauter, come back to see me along with a list of those officers names and we'll review their timecards together."

Ernie Sauter stood, offered his limp hand, mumbled something unintelligible and backed wide-eyed out of the door with his head hung much lower than when he'd first entered the office. Lloyd immediately immersed his head in the filing cabinet to conceal a brief, triumphant grin. He really didn't get much chance to gloat so he wanted to ensure that it was done in complete privacy. The Chief made a mental note to find out which supervisor had been involved with this issue as that person definitely had his or her head on straight and might have promotion potential.

Late in the afternoon he was unexpectedly called to Webster's office. But of course that goes without saying because if it had been expected then he'd have already been there and wouldn't have required calling.

Webster commenced the impromptu meeting with a very serious tone, which really caught Canard by surprise and made him feel quite vulnerable. He supposed that the cashier's allegations had not yet been cleared up or that some new twist had emerged among the evil drunkard's lies.

Then to make things even weirder, Mr. Webster began apologizing. "I'm so sorry I misinterpreted your communication Chief. I've had training for these things yet I completely missed the signs when you approached me yesterday."

He remained silent in hopes that Mr. Webster would shed a little more light on what it was he felt compelled to apologize for so profusely. When that didn't work he confessed blankly, "I have no idea what you are talking about Mr. Webster."

"It's okay Canard. You're in a safe place now," Webster assured.

"I'm not so sure about that," he responded softly as he leaned back in his chair to create a little more distance between his maniac boss and himself.

"My secretary is holding all calls and I've got as much time as this takes," explained Mr. Webster slowly and in a forced rendition of a comforting voice which was very much unlike his usual nasally whine, "You just get comfortable and tell me all about it."

"I don't know what you are asking."

"Just tell me what's on your mind."

"Really?" inquired Lloyd suspiciously. Clearly he was missing something here, but he could not for the life of him figure out what this was about.

"Where to begin?" he joked with a sort of uncomfortable chuckle as he wracked his brain to try to figure out where this odd behavior was coming from.

"You should probably begin with what you wanted to talk to me about yesterday?"

"Yesterday?" he repeated with inflection.

"Yes, that's right.  Yesterday morning when you asked me to have coffee with you."

Lloyd blinked in rapid succession as he recalled the previous uncomfortable visit to Webster's office, then attempted to explain, "I wasn't actually suggesting that we have coffee together, I was just asking if you wanted coffee because I really needed some at that time."

"C'mon Canard," urged Webster gently, "stop hiding behind that tough jarhead exterior and tell me what's really on your mind."

He could see now that Mr. Webster was not simply being randomly idiotic, but that he had some type of goal or direction he expected to go with the weird, uncomfortable scenario he was creating in his office.  His confusion cleared slightly as his concern moved to whether his boss might be experiencing a gay moment. He had previously had his doubts about Webster's personal preferences, but this was the first time that he felt uncomfortably concerned that his supervisor might be looking at him as a possible accomplice.  Lloyd would not have gone so far as to insist that he was the most perfect specimen of a man, but he was positively all hetero without any doubts or lingering curiosities.

The Chief shifted uncomfortably in his chair as he felt like he was on the spot here.  He'd run out of ideas how to tactfully get out of this extremely awkward situation, so now he just stared at his boss blankly.  He didn't want to respond in an undiplomatic manner and really just wanted to get out of his office with the least possible words having to be said.

The silence was broken when Webster suggested, "Tear down that wall you're hiding behind and tell me the truth.  We both know that offering me a cup of coffee was nothing more than a ruse.  Your coy method of letting me know you wanted a little one-on-one time."

"What?!" he blurted in a less than polite manner.

"Yesterday you gave me signals that you wanted something from me; now I'm ready to give you all that you need Lloyd" Webster responded caringly, now on a first name basis.

"Mr. Webster," Canard said with frustration in his voice, "did you call me in here to ask about something important or is this solely about my mention of coffee yesterday?"

"Call me Steve."

"Excuse me?"

"It's okay Lloyd.  Right now I know it is important that you see me more as a friend than a superior.  Go ahead and call me Steve."

"No thanks."

"Really, I think it will make the next step so much easier if you can relax and try to picture to two of us as being equals; side-by-side if you will, and not with me on top like usual" Webster tried to ease his mind.

It didn't work.  Lloyd was now more shaken and discombobulated than ever.

"I really don't think that will be necessary, sir."  He carefully explained, "I'm quite comfortable addressing you as my supervisor.  Which is, by the way, the only way I see you."

"If you insist" Webster conceded.  "The most important thing is that we are able to communicate.  I want you to open up about your thoughts and feelings."

"I really have nothing to share, sir.  The fact is, I rarely share any of my personal thoughts with my wife" he intentionally reminded his boss that he was a married man.

"Well, nonetheless, I am sorry I didn't catch the hint at the time" Webster apologized again.  "But I was distracted.  I accept full responsibility for my error and I really want the chance to help you now."

"Help me with what?" Canard questioned with even more frustration now that the V.P. seemed to imply that his gay proposition was somehow an offer to help.

"With your problem" Webster answered unhelpfully.

"*My* problem?" he tried to understand this twisted man's even more twisted logic.  How could Webster contort Lloyd's boring, normal sexuality to mean that it was he who had the problem and required some kind of perverse assistance to overcome it?

"What problem do I have?" responded Canard in a less patient tone now.

"You haven't told me yet," Webster reminded him with a slight grin of superiority.

"Mr. Webster I have not the faintest clue as to what you are going on about," Canard confessed.

"I recognize that you really didn't want coffee that morning Lloyd" Webster explained knowingly. "You were just using that as an excuse to get me into a one-on-one conversation so you could ask for help. I don't know exactly what's bothering you, but I can see that you are at the end of your rope and nearing the point where your next step will be drastic and possibly life threatening."

"What?!" was all Canard could muster at this point as he was completely put off by his boss's perverted intervention with an apparent hope of turning him.

"I'm offering to help you Lloyd," Webster said almost begging. "I know you were using that excuse about coffee as a shield to cover your cry for help."

"My..." Lloyd began, and then paused as he attempted to understand what he had just heard. He finally finished weakly, "My cry for help?"

They both sat silently for a moment: Lloyd was stunned and confused by the expression on Webster's face as he leaned forward in his chair in an obvious attempt to feign sincere concern.

"You cannot be serious, sir," Lloyd responded. "Is that really why you called me here this morning? To try and convince me that I didn't want coffee but actually wanted to ask you for some kind of help???"

"Now there is no need to get embarrassed Canard," Webster scolded lightly, "I really am offering to help you."

"I can't imagine that you are serious" Canard exclaimed; becoming a bit excited at the absolute absurdity of this situation now.

"I am completely serious Canard" he began, and then softened his approach. "Lloyd, I understand you are in serious need of a friend to help you through this."

"May I be excused to go look for one?" Lloyd inquired bluntly.

Webster exhibited a confused look as Canard's attempt at humor whizzed over his head.

"Look," began Lloyd before pausing to close his eyes and exhale loudly in an exercise to remain calm. "I do not want help. I do not need help. I only wanted a cup of coffee. I like coffee; drink it every day; and yesterday's abhorrent allegations not only hit prior to my first cup, but also greatly increased my need for it."

Webster stared at Chief Canard for a moment as if trying to interpret what it meant when a subordinate asserted that he neither wanted nor needed help. Lloyd remained quiet as he allowed his simple-minded supervisor to work through this confusion which obviously overwhelmed his reasoning capacity.

Finally Webster conceded, "If you're sure I cannot offer any assistance...well, then I guess we're through here."

He could clearly see the defeat showing on Mr. Webster's face as well as hear it in his whiney voice. Canard did not find it comforting that his boss was so disappointed by the fact that he apparently was not desperately crying for help and teetering on the verge of suicide.

As Lloyd walked back towards his office he questioned whether there truly was any conceivable design to the universe. If life was truly so random why did he clearly seem to receive an inordinate share of bad luck? Why did some people appear to lead such charmed lives while others, principally himself, seem to struggle with every situation, every step of the way? If there did indeed exist some form of a deity overseer, then where did he or she spend most of his or her time? Was life so full of cock-ups and disarray by design or was it a result of serious neglect? Lloyd had no chance of ever finding these answers and since the prognosis wasn't consoling he tried not to dwell on these thoughts any longer.

Lloyd missed the order of his days in the Marine Corps. All of his fondest memories were from that era in his life. That this period coincided with his youth and bachelor days was probably a factor as well. The decision-less days of national service as a young enlisted man were simple, effortless times. Certainly not effortless physically; but mentally it wasn't cumbersome at all. As a civilian and an adult, things were much harder. You had to get yourself up in the morning, decide what to wear and then make your own way to work on time. As a young Marine you had no responsibilities other than doing what you were told: you got up when they yelled at you or threw you out of the bunk; you dressed in the exact same clothing every day; and they shouted at you all the way to work even reminding you which foot to put in front of the other. You had no schedule, no clocks or timetables and no paperwork. Someone else took care of those things. You only had to do what you were told, how you were told, until you were eventually ordered to stop.  All thinking and planning was accomplished by unseen forces above your pay grade and the men on the bottom rung only needed adhere with strict obedience to orders, no matter how dangerous or insane, to receive meritorious commendation.

The civilian and military worlds were topsy-turvy and appeared to Canard to be almost completely oblique inverse dimensions.  It was not easy for a man who had spent two decades in one system to transition into the opposite.  Military promotions were based on proven ability.  On the civilian side they looked more at your grades from school and would eagerly hire and elevate supervisors without any semblance of relative prior experience.  On top of that, their budgets and management plans did not provide any useful training to these supervisory newbies, yet they were expected to fully take over the job from day one.  It was a clear recipe for failure and could possibly even be considered torture for subordinates under some international treaties.

Chief Canard quietly returned to his office with little expectation of salvaging any productive time from what was left of the work day.

* * * *

At the end of the day Lloyd drove home from work in the pouring rain.  It was a really bad storm with thick, low dark clouds, frequent sharp lightning and long rumbling thunder.  This was the kind of storm that went well beyond the spring showers that routinely cause gridlock on the streets of South Florida.  Consequently, traffic was horrible.

He finally arrived home to find a quiet house.  This was a nice thing, but completely unexpected and he knew it would never last.  He had expected to hear the whining of Perla and the bickering of Andi but he couldn't hear a thing beyond the rumbling of thunder and the spattering of wind-blown rain on the windows.  This was certainly odd.  He walked through the entire house.  Finally arriving in the master bedroom, he exasperatingly asked out loud to himself "Where in the world are they?"

Lloyd jumped with surprise when he heard Andi's voice respond, "Right here dad!"

He spun around but still saw no one.  He grabbed the door handle and snatched the closet door open expecting to see Andi, though bewildered about what she'd be doing in there.  The closet was empty.  But her voice had sounded so near.

Again he heard Andi's voice, this time laughing as she said, "No Dad, under here."

He scanned the room and was even more confused when he saw his daughter's arm extended from underneath the bed, waving a hand at him.  Clueless as to what was going, on the only thing he could say was, "So, is your mother under there with you?"

"Of course she is" Andi responded.  "Who do you think drug me under here to hide from the thunderstorm?"  Lloyd could almost hear the sound of Andi rolling her eyes in annoyance.

"No comment" whispered Lloyd as he turned to leave the room.

"I heard that!" snapped Perla from underneath the bed.  Now Lloyd rolled his eyes as he flung the useless response "It was *no comment*, you heard nothing" over his shoulder as he departed the bedroom.  He would never claim that marriage to Perla was boring.  Quite to the contrary; it was consistently unpredictable.

Once the storm passed and Perla came out from under the bed, she found her husband sitting in front of the television.  As usual he had a glass of Scotch on ice and his eyes were glued to The Weather Channel, though his mind doubtlessly wandered elsewhere.

Determined to interrupt his relaxing moment of quiet time, Perla bumped the chair hard with her hip as she passed.  Lloyd grunted with disgust but refused to be drawn into yet another argument about nothing for her personal pleasure.

A few minutes later she returned.  This time Perla exhibited a totally different attitude as she called, "Lloyd" in a sweeter-than-usual voice, "Wud you like chicken casserole for dinner?"

His ears perked up.  "Sure," he responded quickly and with an intentionally sincere tone of appreciation, "that sounds great."

"Okay" was her last word on the way out of the living room.

Lloyd picked up the bottle of Scotch and poured another half glass, then leaned his recliner back to relax before dinner was ready.  He wasn't stupid.  He realized straight away that such an unusual offer from his wife was not the result of mere kindness.  Obviously it was Perla's intention to warm her husband up before trying to get something from him. But since he was the only breadwinner and ultimately paid for everything anyway he figured he'd play along with her bribery attempt if it would lead to a rare home cooked meal.

Sipping Scotch, relaxing and flipping between the news and weather channels Lloyd just sort of spaced out for a while. Eventually he happened to notice the time in the corner of the television screen. He couldn't believe an hour and a half had passed. His stomach growled on cue as soon as this thought passed through his head. Lloyd got up from his chair and headed to the kitchen to fix his plate and get a little more ice for his glass. The kitchen was dark and empty. There was no smell of food present and only a pile of dirty dishes submerged in the sink full of cold, suds barren dishwater. He opened the oven. It was empty and cold. He checked the fridge; there was nothing to be found. What had happened to the food?

So Lloyd trudged up the stairs, fueled by hunger and prodded by alcohol. He peered into the bedroom to find Perla in her usual position: propped up on a pile of pillows watching television and snacking on a rapidly dwindling two pound bag of marshmallows.

Lloyd asked politely, "Excuse me, but where is the food?"

Perla tossed the line, "What food?" back at him.

"The chicken casserole of course."

"We don't have any of dat" responded Perla flatly.

"But you said you were fixing it" countered Lloyd in a confused tone.

"No, you misunderstan' me." Perla yanked the hook and reeled him in with her explanation, "I didn't say I wuz going to cook it, I just ask if ju wud like to have some."

Lloyd was stunned with disappointment and he felt the stirring of anger deep within his center. He could make out his wife's poor attempt to conceal a smirk between her bulging cheeks as her face was eerily lighted by the unsteady glow provided from the flickering television screen. He realized that he had fallen for her evil trick and quietly left the room without another word. He was actually angrier at himself for having been taken by the ploy. Lloyd returned to his La-Z-Boy recliner, poured another drink to quell his growling stomach and passed out twenty minutes later.

## *** DAY FOUR ***

## Thursday

Running late due to traffic and excessive daydreaming, Lloyd was hoping to slip quietly and undetected into his office for an undisturbed morning. He really needed some quiet time to rid himself of the eye-squinting headache he suffered from excessive alcohol consumption on an empty stomach the previous evening. He didn't like drinking alone but his wife drove him to it. Combining Perla's incessant nagging with the fact that she had stopped cooking meals and cleaning the house a few years ago meant that he suffered a great deal of aggravation on top of an extremely poor diet. Sometimes it was difficult for him to deal with the hunger, but he discovered that self pity and alcohol were actually quite filling, although certainly not the core of a very healthy lifestyle.

It's too bad he was so overly stubborn that he wouldn't try to change things. Lloyd was the type of guy to fall down in the mud and remain there for some ridiculously idiotic spiteful reason. Although no one else cared but him, that didn't stop Canard always responding the same way. He would never defend his odd behavior as logical, but he'd lived his life on a straight path; always plowing forward despite obstacles, so he continued his momentum forward into the future with the same ridiculous obsessive compulsion. No, it didn't actually make sense, but that was never his intent anyway. He wasn't stupid enough to think that his conduct was hurting anyone other than himself, but he was definitely stupid enough to continue his own self destructive behavior.

Canard knew as soon as he pulled into the Bitewoody parking lot entrance that a quiet morning was not to be found. There were emergency lights flashing, dozens of improperly parked cars blocking the driveways, a mob of people standing around and several yards of yellow police tape encircling the area. He took a deep breath, closed his eyes and said a little prayer as he exhaled slowly. 'Well,' he thought to himself, 'what could it be this time?' It probably was not a bomb scare because his officers would have moved the crowd away. Most likely an injured pedestrian hit by a car or the more frequent case of someone hurt in a fist fight over a parking spot. It's amazing how many times he'd seen that childishly reactive scenario. But that was about the maturity level of their local customer base.

Lloyd left his car where it was since he couldn't possibly pass through the melee anyway, and proceeded on foot to the scene of the incident. As he pushed his way through the crowd he began to worry. This looked worse than what he'd initially thought. He could see no damaged vehicles or arguing customers. Adding to his confusion was the sight of several of his security officers huddled in a small group some distance away from the action talking quietly amongst themselves.

He noticed that emergency medical personnel had not yet arrived on the scene and no one was attempting to administer first aid. Chief Canard's heartbeat increased when he spotted the small visual barrier which had been constructed from orange traffic cones and black plastic garbage bags to obscure the onlookers' view of the victim.

Lloyd only saw one security officer actually working...and to his surprise this young officer, Adrian Gonzalo, was soaked in his own sweat as he frantically performed the work of at least four officers. He briskly approached Gonzalo to determine what exactly was going on. Amazingly, Lloyd thought he heard laughter coming from the huddled group of officers, but when he turned quickly to look at them he heard it no more and they were huddled even tighter. When he reached Gonzalo the expeditious officer was excitedly talking on the radio so rather than interrupt him, Lloyd decided to take a quick look behind the impromptu cover.

Lloyd froze in place. His stomach twisted into a tight knot, his mouth went dry and the sweat underneath his clothes suddenly felt icy cold. The victim under the garbage bag was so small that it was evidently a child, and a very small one at that. He felt physically sick. He quickly scanned for a hysterical, grieving parent but saw no one to fit that description. As he scanned the area, his revulsion and feeling of helplessness quickly turned to anger when he once again saw the group of gawking officers huddled together peering toward him with what appeared to be smirks and grins across several faces.  That was it, he could handle no more.

Forgetting the pain in his throbbing temples, Lloyd raised his voice and yelled at the group of apparently incompetent officers and they rushed towards him now completely smile-free.  When they assembled in front of him, Canard could hold back no longer: "What the hell are you doing?  Don't you understand we've got a major incident here??!!  I saw you all over there laughing like a bunch of idiotic fools!  Has anyone tried to find the mother?"

The officers' faces reflected confusion rather than fear of their boss or comprehension of the situation.

Lloyd was incredulous.  "Are you all high?" he screamed.  "What in the world is happening here?"

One of the officers whispered, "Someone ran over a cat."

Everyone else remained quiet, as was Lloyd while he tried to interpret what this seemingly irrelevant piece of information meant.  It was now the Chief's face that twisted with confusion as he asked a barely audible, "What?"

The timid officer spoke again, "Yes sir, Chief Canard, someone ran over a cat and Gonzalo activated the emergency response procedures."

He felt his jaw dropping toward the ground but was unable to move his hands to catch it.  Before he could catch his breath and respond another officer added, "Actually it happened a couple days ago...I've seen that dead cat here for at least two days prior to this morning."

Lloyd's voice returned, and how: "Are you telling me that there is a two-day-old cat carcass under that garbage bag?"

The officers all shook their heads in confirmation, but no one spoke.

"And what the hell is Gonzalo doing?" he asked them in desperation.

Someone in the back of the small crowd answered, "He's trying to convince the paramedics to make an attempt to revive the cat."

"What?!!" exclaimed Lloyd.  "Why haven't you stopped him?"

"Well, you know Adrian Gonzalo..." someone started, but was quickly interrupted by the Chief's howled response, "No, I do not know Adrian Gonzalo and I certainly will not have time to get to know him!"

Canard then began barking instructions to the officers: "Take that radio away from Officer Gonzalo and call off all responding officers, ambulances and whatever else that idiot has put in a call for! Then get the traffic cleared out and the parking lot back open for business." Then he stated out loud mostly as a personal motivator, "I've got an urgent meeting with Gonzalo."

As he turned from the group of officers and was about to make Gonzalo's day take a turn for the worse, Canard heard someone behind him ask, "So...what do we do with the cat?"

He spun around and asked incredulously, "What?!"

The female officer now regretted asking that question out loud and tried to explain herself by reasoning, "Well, we can't just leave it there can we?"

Lloyd was overwhelmed by a variety of feelings enhanced by the prior evening's excesses and he felt that the best therapy for him would be to wrap his hands around someone's neck.

"I don't care what you do with it, just do it fast!" he answered as he turned to march back towards Officer Gonzalo. He took four steps and then looked back over his shoulder to see the inept officers hadn't yet moved an inch. Lloyd spun to face them, grimaced what he hoped was a most hateful look, and then marched quickly over to the deceased animal. He grabbed the garbage bag covering the cat and used it to scoop up the stiff carcass of the furry, lifeless creature. "Now get this place open and running!!" he screamed back at the immobile gaggle of officers.

As Canard picked up his pace with greater determination to get his hands on Officer Gonzalo, he heard the multiple gasps from the curious crowd gathered around. Then a few people even made loud comments such as, "What do you think you are doing?" followed by an accusation of: "You killer," and, "Oh my God, how barbaric!" Someone even shouted the ridiculous admonition, "Hey, give the poor cat a chance."

Oh how Lloyd despised the brainlessly moronic liberal majority in this community. Their endless hypocritical whining combined with almost absolute refusal to actually do anything positive for their neighbor, community or country just made him want to puke. It was at this point which he realized his anger was too extreme to go through with the desired 'meeting' with Gonzalo...lest the young officer was to be the next carcass laid out in the B.E.O.T.C.H. parking lot. Definitely not with this crowd of pre-packaged hostile witnesses already gathered around.

Ignoring the sneers and accusations from the crowd and with a tightened grip on the stiff animal in his right hand, Lloyd went up to Gonzalo and placed his face just inches from the officer's face. With their noses almost touching the Chief said simply, "Do not speak. Don't say a single word. Just follow me to my car, drop all your crap in my trunk, leave the premises and do not ever return."

Fortunately Gonzalo knew better than to risk a verbal response at this point. He followed his fuming boss to the car, quietly deposited his radio, baton, cap, uniform shirt, and duty belt into the trunk. He then solemnly removed his employee identification badge and whistle, offering them reverently to Chief Canard with his head bowed. Lloyd was disgusted with him and to make that point without physically hurting the idiotic former security officer, he slapped the badge and whistle from Gonzalo's hands where they landed in the trunk, then tossed the garbage bag containing the dead cat in on top of everything else and slammed the door shut.

Having disposed of Gonzalo without killing or seriously harming him had been a challenge. Now Lloyd sat in his car, windows closed, with the air conditioner turned low and the radio playing loudly. He knew this wouldn't help his headache, but just felt he needed to fight pain with pain and hopefully distract himself temporarily from the tragedy of overly-motivated, under-educated, imbecilic, rent-a-cop, law enforcement wannabes.

Once the traffic finally cleared, Lloyd parked his car and headed inside. He filled his cup with coffee, closed the door, sat down at his desk and switched on his computer. While perusing the previous day's paperwork and his appointment calendar, he quickly polished the brass buckle on his belt and lightly buff-shined his shoes. He then brushed his teeth, spitting into the trash can. Having completed his morning rituals in privacy, he opened his office door, sat back down at his desk then grabbed his cup of coffee to wash down a couple aspirin. Lloyd immediately regretted brushing his teeth right before having more coffee. What a disgusting taste! Mistakes and regrets were things he was very well accustomed to, so he cleared the grimace and took another large sip with the intent of washing out the toothpaste and restoring his taste buds to their normal state so he could try to enjoy the remainder of his morning coffee.

Lloyd had missed the 8:15 AM meeting while dealing with the fake emergency in the parking lot. As much as he despised that meeting he couldn't even enjoy the fact that he'd legitimately missed this one because the mess Gonzalo had caused was even more of a headache than listening to Mr. Bitewoody's stupid pool stories. He settled in his office to try to get some work done. Opening his email he quickly realized that this morning's cat incident was big news in the rumor mill and had evidently spread quite widely throughout the entire organization. It pissed him off even more to see that the flow of rumors was creating a tidal wave of anger directed at him. Somehow the screwball masses had decided that it was actually Canard who had murdered the cat.

There was a massive influx of hate mail about him, but not intentionally sent directly to him. Ridiculously, his idiotic coworkers managed to include him on the mailing list of each message. Once the first goofball did it, everyone else unthinkingly pressed 'reply all' and his inbox was under siege. Lloyd knew that he should simply delete this mindlessly mailed crap, but his curiosity got the best of him and he skimmed most of it. Well aware that curiosity had killed the proverbial cat, he still thought that the best way to manage a strong defense against this mounting hatred orchestrated towards him was to be fully aware of the hate filled comments, nicknames, threats and goings on. He made the decision to try to stay out of sight as much as possible for the remainder of the day. Venturing into the hallways filled with angry people probably wouldn't be the best move right now. The Chief was learning a lot more than he wanted to know about the depravity of his coworkers. In addition to the emails, his office phone rang much more than usual with annoying and anonymous calls suggesting a variety of places where he should go and an assortment of creatively vulgar things he should do to himself once he got there.

Lloyd was able to spend the majority of the day secluded in his office even skipping lunch and grabbing a series of short, but non-refreshing naps.  His head still hurt, he was very hungry, but he was thinking mostly of just getting home and plopping into bed before Perla could start in on him as well.  Between the dwindling headache he still carried from downing most of that bottle of Scotch last night and the fresh headache that was still sprouting up from the idiotic actions of that imbecile Gonzalo, he had every intention of taking off earlier than usual today.  Unfortunately, just like every other plan he made, something came up that prevented his much-needed escape.

Closing his eyes and exhaling deeply while his computer was shutting down, Lloyd said a silent prayer for a better tomorrow.  As if in response to his prayer, in walked Liz Jordan.  But the tidings she carried were not of joy: "Mr. Webster needs to like, see you in his office" she proclaimed.  Miss Jordan glanced conspicuously at Canard's phone and added "Mr. Webster said he called you several times but you like, never answered."

"Really?" Lloyd faked surprise then looked down at his phone and responded, "Oh, I see what happened.  Looks like I accidentally kicked the cord and unplugged it from the wall."

"Okay Mr. Canard" was Liz's reply in a tone indicating complete disbelief.  As she turned to leave the office she reminded her boss, "Just don't forget to see Mr. Webster, because *I answered* his call and like, told him you *were* actually still here." His headache delivered a sharp stabbing pain behind his brow as if deliberately accentuating the bad news Liz had just rendered.

"Yeah, okay," he responded in serene surrender, "good night Liz."

He pondered quietly on what Vice President Webster could possibly need to see him about so late in the workday.  It was really no use trying to guess as it seemed that Mr. Webster was capable of drawing upon an endless source of stupid suggestions and bad ideas.  He closed his eyes in desperate need of relief as he opened his mouth and worked his jaw several times.  He sometimes felt pain in his jaw when the stress was greater than usual.  Canard assumed he unconsciously tensed in these areas as he tried to hold himself back from saying the things he wished or responding in a more violent way when things went wrong.  He had learned to expect the unexpected and knew that his only luck was bad luck.  Although Canard was an admitted pessimist and therefore actually expected bad things to happen, the practice did not ultimately offer any relief from the resulting pain and aggravation when his premonitions repeatedly came true.  So he reluctantly went to the vice president's office with the hope of quickly getting through whatever new torture his boss had devised.

"Chief Canard, come in please" invited Mr. Webster.

"Yes sir, what can I do for you?" inquired Lloyd wanting to get directly to the point.

"It's about this cat business Chief," Webster began, "this thing has become somewhat of a larger incident than I had expected and I'm trying to find the best way out of it."

"I agree with you sir, people have really gone crazy over this thing" answered Lloyd.  "But I think it's just another brief fad that will blow over and be forgotten in a couple days."

"I don't know Chief," the V.P. hesitated, "I've had some pretty strong complaints about your actions and there are some extremely high emotions involved here.  Several employees have already requested sick leave to deal with a death on the premises; and those aren't even the ones I'm most concerned about."  Lloyd shook his head in amazement and commented, "Wow, these people will use any excuse won't they?" then finished with a laugh.

"I don't think it's a laughing matter Canard" Webster told him bluntly.  "I have heard of more than a few credible threats against you and frankly I'm concerned about our liability."

"And your safety of course" Webster added as an afterthought.  "Anyway, I think you need a break from this place."

"So, you want me to take some time off?"  Lloyd asked curiously.

"Not necessarily..." Webster began.

Lloyd cut him off "But sir, that cat was killed at least two days before Gonzalo came upon the alleged crime scene."

"Really?" asked Webster with sincere surprise.  "So do you know who did it?"

He looked at his boss incredulously for a moment then responded, "No sir.  All we know for sure is that the cat's body was cold, stiff and thoroughly lifeless well before Officer Gonzalo pulled that ridiculous attempt to revive the damned thing this morning."

"Well at least you've made progress on pinpointing the time of the unscrupulous attack" Webster praised.  "Hopefully Brittle will prove to be as capable in taking over the investigation and tracking down the culprit."

Lloyd wasn't sure how to respond to the two revelations from his boss's last statement.  Should he be more concerned that his boss actually thought he was conducting a criminal investigation on the flat cat or that Mr. Webster made a clear reference to Assistant Chief Brittle 'taking over' for him?

So he asked simply, "What do you want me to do?"

"I've decided to send you on a training assignment" he explained.  "I think this will kill two birds with one stone."  Webster winced in horror then quickly apologized, "I'm sorry Canard.  I didn't think before saying that.  I realize you've witnessed enough death recently without my uncompassionate conjuring up even more images."  Vice President Steve Webster glanced around the room suspiciously then concluded, "We really have to be careful with slip ups like that since these animal rights activists are extremely sensitive."

"Mentally encumbered with overly emotional, irrational reactions is how I'd classify it" Lloyd exclaimed; hoping desperately to find an ally in his boss.  Instead Webster stared blankly at the Chief as his mind pondered what business school Canard might have attended.

Canard kept silent as he wondered whether he was the subject of a prank or if his boss was truly as stupid as he appeared.  He looked slowly around the room for evidence of hidden cameras because he was almost sure that they were having him on and probably recording this for some type of candid camera episode.  Mr. Webster's face revealed only concern and no hint of joking.  He was in near disbelief as he observed the vice president clearly grieving the loss of the stray.  This particular reality was much worse than being the subject of some elaborate practical joke.

Once again he had that familiar feeling of being surrounded by idiots.  Canard didn't believe that he suffered some form of superiority complex because he knew better than anyone his own plethora of shortcomings, faults and failures.  It was just that he so often felt like he was sinking in a sea of dumbasses at work.  An unceasing morass of dumbass as it were.

"What's the assignment then?" he asked brusquely through his tightening jaws.

Mr. Webster lifted a folder from his desk and handed it to him without revealing any specifics. "This contains your schedule, tickets and all reservations."

Canard exhaled loudly as he leaned back in the chair and opened the folder. A quick review of the contents explained why the V.P. didn't want to discuss the details.

"A conference?" Lloyd asked out loud. "A three day conference?" he repeated even louder. "In *New York City*?!" he emphasized even more.

"Come on Mr. Webster, what is this?" he pleaded.

"PETA" was Webster's one word response.

"Peter?" asked Canard. "Peter who?"

"It's not a who," explained Webster, "it's an organization, People for the Ethical Treatment of Animals; PETA."

"Oh my God!" he exclaimed in surprise. "Mr. Webster...I don't understand...I don't want..."

"It's pretty simple Chief Canard" Webster said with an unexpected authority as he interrupted Lloyd's protest. "You will go to this conference. It will get you away from Bitewoody Center while things cool down as well as provide clear proof to employees and the public that this organization supports animal rights and never condones the mistreatment of any of our fellow creatures."

Mr. Webster stood to indicate the meeting was over and delivered his final instructions, "Your plane leaves in less than three hours so you have to hurry. I tried to inform you earlier, but I was unable to reach you." Lloyd stood up and left his boss's office without another word. Dissension was clearly superfluous at this point and he had a flight to catch.

Having received the surprise special assignment Lloyd now suffered a new pain...his teeth hurt. This was a phenomenon he suffered very rarely when under extreme stress. He knew it wasn't a good sign, but he certainly understood why he was feeling it now. New York City: the bastion of unthinking liberal veneration. The land where the masses revere the motto of no responsibility for self and absolutely no consideration of others. Where a man can be a man, but also not be, almost simultaneously. He recalled the time he'd stumbled upon a reality show about how the prevalence of cross-dressing was changing the already seedy nightlife in New York one evening when he was flipping channels. It was one of those revelations that strike so unexpectedly that a person finds it extremely difficult to look away. In face he'd watched twenty minutes of the show before snapping out of the tranny trance and clicking the remote in a useless attempt to erase the unsettling education he'd just received. New York was a city revered by most of the outside world as an exemplary model of America's greatness, while at the same time served as fertile ground for America's newest fad of self deprecation; in which patriotism had curiously been redefined as unrestrained disdain of one's own country.

"God Bless America and deliver us from New York City!" Lloyd delivered out loud in the empty hallway. He couldn't recall if that was a quote he'd heard somewhere before or if the sentiment had just popped into his head. He knew for certain that he'd stick out like a sore thumb up there. He could only imagine the conflicts that might arise from a man such as himself from an ultra-rural, largely conservative background being thrust into the jungle-like atmosphere of the big city. Being a military veteran from North Carolina with a background in law enforcement and physical security couldn't possibly win him any friends there either. In his mind the impending scene resembled that of chum being dangled over the water to entice a frenzy among the circling sharks. The rampant crime, the flagrant perversion and the unabashed rudeness would probably do him in for good.

Lloyd thought to himself that he should be accustomed to being an outsider by now. That's practically how he'd felt most of his life. No matter where he was or what he was doing he always seemed to be separated from the people around him. Sometimes the gap was very thin, but other times the space was humongous. So, since he often felt without an ally or confidant, he usually kept his thoughts, irreverent comebacks and irrelevant observations quietly to himself. He handled frequent disappointments, frustration and anger the same way. He was aware that bottling up these fierce emotions was not a healthy response, but he didn't know what else to do. Letting loose his frustrations on the tormenters causing them would surely result in a worse outcome and very possibly land him in prison for a long time. So Lloyd sucked it up, pushed it down deep inside and carried on as best he could with his ever increasing burden.

The last minute assignment to attend the conference didn't put Lloyd in a complete bind as he had learned from his military days to always keep a bag packed with extra clothing and basic toiletries. Though he was no longer accustomed to the night time drills and surprise deployments, Lloyd did still maintain a duffel bag in the trunk of his car. If nothing else it gave him the mental comfort of being prepared to run away from his unhappy life at a moment's notice. Though he really had no idea what type of notice, or from where it might actually arise, could possibly lead him to such a drastic act. As stupid an idea as it was, a desperate man needs some illusion of hope even if it is a ridiculous long shot dream.

Before leaving for the airport Lloyd returned to his office to make a quick call home. The phone rang several times before someone finally answered it with a dull, "Hello?"

"Hey Andi, its Dad. Is your mother around?" Lloyd asked.

"I think so," Andi responded. "But I think she's sleeping."

"Sleeping?" Lloyd pondered out loud. "At 3:30 in the afternoon?"

"I dunno" replied Andi.

"You don't know what?"

"Huh?"

"I asked, what it is that you said you don't know?"

"What?" asked Andi with only a slightly curious inflection.

Lloyd raised his voice a little, "Do you know if she's sleeping or not?!!"

"I told you I think she's sleeping" Andi came back with a disrespectful tone.

"You also told me that you didn't know if she was sleeping," Lloyd uselessly tried to reason with his daughter.

"I don't know what you're talking about" Andi said in a voice which indicated both her lack of respect and a complete void of interest in her father's questions.

"What are you doing now?"

"What?"

"I asked what are you doing right now?" Lloyd repeated slower and a bit louder.

"Talking to you" Andi responded with obvious annoyance and complete disinterest.

"Are you watching TV?"

"Yeah."

"Yes sir" corrected Lloyd.

"What?"

"Sir!" Lloyd counseled better manners once again.

"Huh? Are you talking to me or someone else?" Andi asked in a belligerent tone she tried to disguise as being confused.

"Yes, I'm talking to you Andi" Lloyd said in a frustrated voice. "At least that's what I was trying to do."

"What do you want?" Andi finally posed bluntly as if she was clueless to anything that had previously occurred.

Lloyd exhaled loudly and changed the subject. "Do you have any homework?"

"I dunno."

What do you mean you don't know?"

"I don't remember. I have to check" was Andi's poor attempt at an explanation.

"Well you need to go ahead and get started Andi" he instructed uselessly. He already knew his daughter would ignore him just as she'd learned to do from her mother's example.

"And tell your mother that I have to go to a conference in New York. I'll be back in about three days" Lloyd informed his distracted daughter.

"Uh huh" was the only response Andi offered.

Lloyd ended the call without another word as he accepted the realization that the television set had once again won the battle for his daughter's attention.

On his way to the airport Lloyd was able to see a brighter side of this current dilemma. Any three day break from the office was a relief...even if it was actually under the guise of punishment. And if the pretext of punishment was what it took to get paid time away from that crazy place then screw it. Pressure in the office would certainly be more than that at an animal lover's conference. Besides, it would probably be a great idea to avoid the office while things cooled down from the incident. "*The incident*!!" Lloyd said out loud to accentuate the fatuity of the whole ordeal. How could things have reached a point where an anonymous dead cat in the parking lot could possibly rise to the level of such a serious incident? It seemed to Canard that the only thing capable of shaking the South Florida liberal population from their laissez-faire attitude was the idea of some animal being mistreated. These people appeared to be in a continually running competition to see who could come up with the most ridiculous campaign behind which to focus their irrational enthusiasm. It was a shame that their motivation couldn't be harnessed to concentrate on an important issue such as children's education, traffic management, local garbage cleanup, improved public safety issues or anything that might ultimately provide some real benefit to the community. They certainly never seemed capable of organizing and following through on any issue that might actually improve the lives of ordinary people or even benefit their pets for that matter. What a joke it had all become...although it was sometimes very hard to laugh.

Arriving at the airport, Lloyd had the pleasure of dealing with unruly crowds of people that refused to walk on the right and insisted on repeatedly stopping in the walkways to check their watches or talk on their cell phones while leaving their oversized bags blocking the narrow aisles between the overpriced shops and the rarely staffed customer service counters. Airports have long been a place for people to showcase their ignorance and absolute worst behavior. Combine that with the normal frustrations of travel, ever-changing security requirements, lack of manners and the nearly nonexistent customer service and you have a cauldron filled with the boiling stew of stupidity just waiting for the next idiot to bump the stove and disgorge the toxic contents.

On top of all that, Lloyd had the incredible fortune of being assisted by a horribly anti-social ticket agent. Cynthia, as her nametag read, was absolutely the worst sort of person you'd want to have representing your company to the public. But here she was in all her customer-hating glory, dishing it out to anyone unlucky enough to be served by her. He didn't argue. He was accustomed to this bastardized form of customer service in most places around South Florida. Besides, in reality Cynthia's rude behavior and belittling treatment was the best interaction he'd had with anyone all day. It was easier to dismiss the actions of the ticket agent because he understood that she treated everyone that way. So in this case at least, it wasn't intended to be a personal attack on him. Lloyd was also slightly amused with his own reminiscence of the days when ugly women like Cynthia would try much harder to be nice. With an absence of looks the homely ones like Cynthia would usually endeavor to cultivate attractive personalities. Lloyd didn't think that this shift was purely a result of the women's liberation movement. No, this was different and much larger than one disgruntled, homely airline ticket agent. Nowadays most people didn't care a lick about anyone else in the world at all and this unhappy Delta Airlines ticket agent named Cynthia might as well have been their representative.

He was disappointed by society's prevailing attitudes these days. Canard was basically a very simple man; devoid any interest in competing with neighbors or trying to impress strangers through the worship of fads and newfangled gadgetry. He no longer paid much attention to politics, since he was largely unable to notice a difference between parties or candidates, and he could not long tolerate the stridently treacherous dishonesty of nearly every one of the narcissistic participants. In any case, Canard's own life provided enough drama, worry and crises to keep him sufficiently occupied. He lived his life without any desire or expectation of acknowledgment, promotion or award. Sure, he led a life full of surprises, but they were hardly ever the good kind. The only recognition available in his life was for manhandling drunk cashiers and abusing dead cats. These sorts of things were the highlights of his existence and Lloyd had learned to expect nothing more from life.

\* \* \* \*

He was feeling a little better now: out of the office, away from the hateful stares, and intentionally loudly whispered comments and taunts. Sure the airport was crowded, but in the horde of strangers he just blended in and enjoyed the anonymity. Lloyd was determined to simply zone out on this trip. He decided that he would make the best of this break from Bitewoody. This conference was bogus. It was nothing he'd have to participate in or report on and zilch he would really have to pay that much attention to. Heck, he might just blow off the conference altogether, sleep late and instead go sightseeing around the Big Apple.

After getting his boarding pass and checking his suitcase, Lloyd proceeded to queue for security screening. This line moved a bit slower, but at least things were calm. Finally reaching the front, he approached the two Transportation Security Administration screeners when they signaled simultaneously. The first instructed him, "Empty your pockets," while the second officer followed immediately with "Place your bag on the conveyor belt." They seemed oblivious to the fact that a second person was also giving orders and each was perturbed that Lloyd seemed to be doing something other than what he was being told. The first officer then reminded him "Remove your belt, watch and any other jewelry." The second fellow began talking before the first guy finished, "Take your shoes off and put them in the gray bin." Lloyd was annoyed at having two different TSA screeners concurrently give him varying instructions, but he attempted to comply so as to get through the ordeal as quickly as possible. As he bent over to unlace his shoes he heard someone ask "What gate are you going to?" He was stooped forward so he turned his head slightly and answered over his shoulder, "It's C-4," then went back to the task of removing his shoes. No sooner had Lloyd resumed unlacing his shoes, he was hit hard from behind without any warning at all. There was a lot of shouting in the background as he was crumpled helplessly on the floor before he even realized he had been struck. He was disoriented for several seconds as he tried to understand what was happening. The only things he knew for sure were that something had occurred which both obscured his vision and resulted in his complete inability to move any portion of his body.

Canard's takedown was initiated by a highly motivated, recently hired TSA officer on roving patrol who was just passing by the screening station at precisely the most inopportune moment. While this young security officer had no law enforcement or military experience, he definitely considered himself to be totally 'hard core.' Unfortunately this young fellow was a bit too high strung with gung ho fever and when he heard Canard give his response to the gate inquiry he reacted. The combination of hearing the term 'C-4' and observing the passenger reaching down for his shoe was too much for the undertrained brain of the rookie officer and he quickly jumped on the suspicious subject's back. The young officer's mind was absent of any concerns about there being an actual explosive device in the suspect's shoe, but filled only with the image of himself being awarded the Congressional Medal of Honor by the President of the United States on the Oprah Show in front of a wildly appreciative America.

After the first TSA officer tackled Lloyd it was only a natural reaction by the other bored security officers to not miss out on an opportunity to pummel a traveler. With luck, they thought, they might just discover a terrorist at the bottom of the pile. But if nothing else, at least they would have that awesome tackle to brag about after an otherwise uneventful shift. It took a couple minutes before the stack of elbow swinging officers was removed and the confused Canard was found at the bottom of the pile holding his boarding pass in one hand and a shoe in the other. He and his luggage were moved to a small side room and another embarrassing fifteen minutes passed as he was stripped naked and all his belongings were dumped on the floor subject to additional security inspections. While these nuisance searches were being conducted a more astute supervisor talked to the officers at the checkpoint and reviewed the video tape to conclude that Canard was actually not at fault. Realizing the confusion, the TSA supervisor immediately instructed his officers to cease harassing the traveler and allow him to dress and repack his bag. Both the supervisor and the young officer apologized for the incident. As an extra measure of precaution to protect his own position from a possible legal response by the perturbed passenger, the supervisor fired the incapable officer on the spot. This did make Lloyd feel a little bit better as he was sadly all too accustomed to dealing with the same level of employees. Once he had gathered his things, he quickly departed the area and went in search of his departure gate. As he walked through the airport, Lloyd considered the obviously bad idea of having named a secure zone of the airport after a military grade explosive popular with radicals and insurgents. Canard thought the airport authorities should take a hint from those people responsible for labeling hotel floors and skip over Gate C-4 as they routinely did with floor thirteen.

Lloyd finally made it aboard the plane of the Delta Airlines subsidiary, but his travel adventures were far from over. He was not only squeezed into a tiny, uncomfortable center seat on the Song aircraft, but he was also endlessly harassed with the rotating message on the small television screen taunting: "More Comfort, More Productivity and no more Middle Seats." He tried to ignore the flagrantly fictitious scrolling message, but the absolute blatant absurdity of the entire advertisement was utterly infuriating. Since he was unable to reach the controls to change the channel or turn the screen off the torture continued. The middle seats claim was an obvious lie as Lloyd was assigned 17B, and was currently jammed between two oversized New Yorkers who were clearly fans of sleeveless shirts, but woefully unfamiliar with the invention of antiperspirant deodorant. With their refusal to share the joint armrests, the men's thick, hairy arms pinned Lloyd's own arms in place by his sides. He was almost completely immobilized by the seating arrangement which had him wedged into a seat too slender to accommodate the hips of an average adult. His shoulders and head were positioned forward of his waistline which meant he had to strain his lower back to prevent falling forward on his face. His knees were jammed against the back of the seat in front of him, in which sat a young man who insisted on continually bouncing in his seat as if in the throes of some lurid act with an invisible partner while straddling the back of a frantically galloping race horse. His husky seatmates insisted on carrying on a conversation as if oblivious to the poor sod stuck in the center. Canard did offer to swap seats so they could converse easier, but they refused that offer flatly as neither of them had any desire to be crammed into that horribly restrictive middle seat. Adding to the aggravation, one of them informed him, "It's not a problem; we don't mind talking a little louder to make up for the distance."

'And More Productivity:' what the hell could that possibly mean? There was no Internet access, no phone service, no power plugs for electronics, no individual reading lamp and even if you could somehow manage to extract a laptop computer from the small storage area by your feet, you'd lose the space required to open it when that inconsiderate bastard sitting in the seat in front of you inevitable decided to perform a surprise power recline. He could not possibly imagine any less comfort unless a third overweight Yankee was squeezed onto his lap to match the two obnoxious sweat-factories hogging the armrests on either side of him now. He began wondering if he might suffer deep vein thrombosis from the extreme discomfort and loss of circulation, but once he remembered that it was fatal, his fears diminished. He was fairly certain fate had no intention of letting him out of this crappy life anytime soon.

During the trip, the flight attendant came around and sat a tiny cup of ice water on the little fold down table on top of Lloyd's knees. Evidently TSA's permitting liquid containers up to three ounces through security didn't affect the airline's decision to use cups of much smaller capacity. The drink was a nice gesture, but

Lloyd's efforts to reach it were futile. With his shoulders pinned in place by his two unpleasant, unyielding seatmates he could move only his forearms. Since he was unable to utilize his arms above the elbows he could not reach out to retrieve the drink. He sat staring at the condensation building up on the outside of the small plastic cup. The specks of water eventually joined and formed drops, which flowed down the outside of the cup as if deliberately teasing him. Watching this only made him feel hotter, thirstier and more aggravated. With quite a bit of strain he was finally able to manipulate the cup closer by carefully bouncing the table with his knees until the cup moved into range of his fingertips. Once he was finally able to grip the cup between the fingertips of both hands, Lloyd bent his neck forward to lower his head as far as possible. Lifting only from his elbows and manipulating the cup with his wrists he was able to uncomfortably manage to take a drink, but not without spilling a small amount. The scene of him drinking in such a ridiculous praying mantis fashion and the fact that much of the water dribbled down his chin where he was unable to wipe it off because his hands were occupied, led onlookers to believe he suffered some sort of mental impairment. He didn't consider how odd he must look until he noticed the stares. Somewhat embarrassed by the situation he decided to forgo the drink and try to take a nap. Although he wasn't able to rest very well he did keep his eyes closed the remainder of the flight.

Upon landing at New York's La Guardia Airport, Lloyd noticed a much more courteous lot of people as they tried to assist him with retrieving his bag from the overhead compartment, asked if he knew where he was going, whether he was traveling alone, if someone was meant to meet him and all sorts of pestering questions in their assumptions that he wasn't quite right and required their unsolicited assistance. Canards unwitting new role was further exacerbated by the fact that having been motionless for the entire three hour flight, his left leg had fallen asleep. This caused him to wobble and wince in pain with each step. The irregular movement and the accompanying facial contortions added to the confusion of his character. So he hurriedly left the gate with a peculiar gait and escaped the audience by quickly ducking into the first men's room he saw and seeking refuge in a stall hoping that the pestering passengers would lose interest in him. He really did have to use the bathroom after the flight, so he just took his time, searched through his bag for the hotel reservation information and then stopped at the sink to wash his face and brush his teeth.

It was while Lloyd was malingering at the sink that he spotted a small child standing alone near the wall by the last toilet stall. He assumed the little boy was waiting for his father. As he was brushing his teeth, he could see pretty clearly that no feet appeared below the stall doors. He scanned to mirror for other signs, but was almost certain that all of the stalls were unoccupied. He watched as the few other patrons in the restroom ignored the child. He had no desire at all to get involved in anything that might delay his arrival at the hotel. After such a long and annoying day, he was eager to take a hot shower and relax in the hotel room. He took his time putting his toiletries back into his duffel bag then slowly washed his face as he contemplated what to do. Regardless of how tired he was Lloyd could not consider neglecting this child who might really need help. Reluctantly he approached the out-of-place boy and asked, "Are you alone young man?" The kid glanced around nervously then lowered his eyes to Lloyd's shoes and replied, "I thought my dad came in here, but now I've been waiting for him a really long time." The child recited this line as if reading a cue card, but Lloyd could tell from the way he continually darted his eyes about the other men in the room that the kid was genuinely nervous and apparently lost.

"Not to worry lad, I'll take care of you" said Lloyd with a friendly smile. Placing a reassuring hand on the boy's shoulder he inquired, "Who's your daddy?" No sooner had the less than soothing connotation barely passed his lips than Lloyd was swarmed, tackled and pushed face-first onto the damp tiled floor of the men's room. His arms were twisted roughly behind his back and the breath was knocked out of him as he was pressed hard into a puddle composed of urine and ammonia. Having someone's sharp, boney knee resting heavily on the back of his neck quelled all attempts he made to replenish his lungs. When he was finally yanked painfully upright by one of the officers, his face was dark blue with lack of oxygen. The cop pushed him forcefully against the wall and demanded: "What were you going to do to that boy?!" Finally able to breathe again Canard was unable to answer, but instead gasped loudly for air and his blue face flushed to bright red with the return of oxygen to his system. The suspect's failure to answer the question combined with his obvious blush faced embarrassment was sufficient evidence of guilt for the officers manning the airport pedophile sting operation. They called in the apprehension of the long sought child molester and signaled the close of the intensive undercover sting operation dubbed 'Bathroom Buddy.'

Lloyd had his arm wrenched painfully behind his back as he was being handcuffed and led from the men's room through the airport and out to a waiting cruiser with lights flashing. It seemed the policemen spared no opportunity to call attention to their presence and the poor slob they had in custody. The prisoner had no choice in the matter and quickly realized his pleas of innocence fell on uninterested ears.

Upon arriving at the police station Lloyd finally asked, "Shouldn't someone read me my rights?"

"Monsters like you shouldn't have rights!" the officer blurted abruptly.

"I can assure you that I am no monster, definitely do have rights and am quite aware that I have neither been informed of said rights nor any charges" Lloyd bravely stated. Then added, "Can someone please tell me what's going on here?"

"As if you didn't know, you pervert" began the same officer in an unprofessional tirade. "You were just snatched up in an undercover operation to get miscreants like you out of the airport restrooms where you stalk your innocent, underage victims."

"What?" shouted Canard. "That's absolutely ridiculous!" He frustratingly attempted to explain, "My intentions were simply to get him home..."

"Yeah, we got that much" interrupted the booking sergeant. "But what were you going to do once you had him at your house?"

"No, you're not understanding me" Lloyd tried desperately to reach these police officers who were suffering extreme tunnel vision. "I wanted to get him to *his* house, not my house."

"So, you intended to burgle as well as bugger?" inquired the officer who insisted on leading this conversation even further away from reality.

"I didn't intend anything other than to assist what I thought was a lost child in reconnecting with his father" Lloyd explained again desperately.

The officer tried again, "And by reconnecting you mean..."

"Jesus man!" shouted Lloyd before the officer could complete his accusation; then asked "Are you completely sick?"

"Are you prepared to make a statement at this time?" broke in the sergeant once again.

"I can't see how my being prepared for anything would make a difference since everything you've done so far has been with the obvious intent of providing me with the most intrusive and inconvenient treatment possible" Lloyd reasoned without hiding his frustration.

The impatient sergeant interrupted with the simple question, "Statement: yes or no?"

Lloyd resumed his long-winded answer, "I don't understand why you continue to ask that ridiculous question when I've already proclaimed my innocence repeatedly without any one of you paying one bit of attention."

"We don't take statements of innocence" explained the fifteen year veteran of the New York City police force. "We only take confessions of guilt."

Canard silently gave the officer a hard look of obvious confusion.

"Everybody we catch makes the same claim of innocence and experience has taught us how to handle this" explained the sergeant. "Since we don't prepare paperwork on people who haven't committed crimes we do not create any documentation until you decide to tell us about your criminal activities. So, unless you are ready to tell us about your disgusting intentions for that little boy then we are through here."

Lloyd's mind reeled with these revelations and he imagined the hundreds or possibly thousands of innocent men and women that had received similarly illegal and unjust treatment before him. With no evident record kept for illegal arrests there was no telling how many people had been railroaded in this same fashion. Based on the statement just made by the sergeant, the New York City jails were quite possibly filled with truly innocent people who had been coerced into false confessions or were being held under lock and key somewhere without any record because they were unwilling to admit to crimes they had not committed. Considering the grave situation in which he found himself and the obvious bias of the police he was dealing with, Canard bit his lip in desperate attempt to hold back the response he really wanted to give. These public servants apparently operated under the belief they could do no wrong and would never be held responsible for such abhorrent actions. He stared incredulously at the ignorant sergeant and thought it better not to reveal what he was really thinking. All he chose to say was, "Well, since you've explained it that way then I certainly have nothing more to say."

"You can play it that way if you want," warned the salty sergeant, "but it'll look worse on your part if you refuse to cooperate."

"Sergeant, I have no desire to make things any more difficult than they have already been" stated Canard quite frankly. "But I did nothing wrong and therefore cannot provide you with a confession of guilt. Should you desire to hear the facts, I will speak to you now, but I can provide nothing more than the honest truth."

"Yeah, yeah...that's what they all say" stated the sergeant as he turned his eyes toward the ceiling in an expression of disbelief. Turning his back on the uncooperative detainee, the sergeant jerked his thumb back over his shoulder and instructed the escorting officer, "Lock him up in isolation cell number three," as he was walking out of the room. Lloyd knew this would be a long night.

A few hours later the same officer returned and without apology unlocked the cell door and told him he could leave. Lloyd's mood quickly ran the span from relief, through the tunnel of confusion, then out into the open range of righteous anger. He demanded to see the booking sergeant.

"He's unavailable" was the only response the officer at the front desk would provide.

"May I please see someone who can explain to me what happened and why I've been mistreated, embarrassed and now released without a word of explanation or anything even remotely resembling an apology?"

"No one here" was the brusque reply from the clearly uninterested officer as he pretended to be distracted with completing paperwork.

"Well I'm not leaving until someone gives me some kind of answers!" exclaimed Lloyd forcefully.

"Suit yourself" said the desk officer with a shrug of indifference. "I just hope they don't change their minds about letting you go."

'Oh hell!' thought Lloyd. 'What if that actually happened?' They had already accosted and abused him, violated his rights and arrested him for nothing; so what was to prevent them from doing it all over again? He wanted to follow through with what he knew was proper and file a complaint, but he also knew that these cops had no qualms about ignoring legal procedures and trumping up charges. So, since he had not actually been charged with anything, he figured maybe he should just cut his losses and get out of there while he could. He knew that with his luck and enough time anything could happen.

It was an annoyed and fatigued Canard that finally arrived at the hotel in the middle of the night. Not surprisingly the agent at the check-in desk couldn't locate his reservation. The rude clerk even accused him of not knowing which hotel he had actually booked. Of course neither the clerk nor the hotel could ever be at fault. Once the reservation was found under 'Gunnard,' it showed that the booking was actually made by the very same desk agent. The unrepentant clerk turned the table and blamed him by explaining quite seriously, "You must have pronounced it wrong." Lloyd stared at the queer little man for a moment then commented, "Yeah, you're right. I do fail to properly enunciate my own name from time to time." It never crossed the clerk's mind to apologize and admit fault. Instead the inept hotel representative took yet another stab at the customer by making the smart-alecky remark, "May I offer you a wake-up call? I'm sure you would benefit from a reminder to get up on the *right* side of the bed tomorrow!" Welcome to New York City! He couldn't believe the clerk's insolence. What had happened to young people to cause them to behave so selfishly and with total disregard for others? It seemed an omen of much worse ahead for our culture and the country overall. Lloyd wasted no further words on the fruity little clerk and simply walked away. He took the elevator to his room on the twelfth floor and made a beeline for the shower. Canard took a long, extra hot shower to extract the grime he'd collected from a long day at Bitewoody, being tackled at Fort Lauderdale Airport, enduring a disgusting flight between two sweaty seatmates, being forced to wallow in puddles of God alone knew what on the floor of the La Guardia Airport bathroom, and spending several hours in the poorly ventilated precinct confinement area where the stagnant smells of urine and vomit had permeated his clothing leaving him with the feeling that he'd soaked his entire body in some ordure scented purée with a texture that clung to his body like thick pond scum.

Once that horrendous chore was done, Lloyd felt so wonderfully refreshed that he didn't even completely dry off before flopping heavily onto the large, fluffy bed and falling into a deep, much needed sleep.

# *** DAY FIVE ***

# Friday

Lloyd was roused from a restful slumber by the slow rolling sound of distant thunder. 'Ah, what a relaxing sound' he thought only slightly conscious. Too relaxed even to peek at the clock, he was comfortable with the simple fact that it was still dark outside. He nestled deeper into the pile of pillows on the king bed he had all to himself and lazily drifted back to sleep. A piercing, high pitched BEEP-BEEP-BEEP-BEEP jerked him abruptly awake. After several confusing seconds of trying to recognize where he was and what he was hearing, Lloyd took a peep out the window. The sound of rolling thunder rumbled once again, but the noise was much less romantic this time as he watched the hydraulic arms of the garbage truck lift another large green dumpster and shake its contents into the cavernous opening of the trailer. As the ugly realism of his life ebbed back into his mind, he considered the probability that he was assigned a room overlooking the dumpsters rather than the garden, swimming pool or even the street. Once his mind began to churn any chance of sleeping in was lost. His thoughts turned inevitably to the conglomeration of events and misunderstandings that had led him to an undesirable hotel room for a conference on animal rights in the bleeding heart of New York City.

Lloyd got up, showered, skipped the shave to emphasize his freedom and then dressed. He struggled to choke down three quarters of a cup of stale hotel room coffee as he thought about the day ahead. His focus was already set on ignoring the conference and simply trying to enjoy some solitude during this rare time away from both work and home. He certainly didn't need to undergo animal sensitivity training anyway. What he truly needed was a break from all the idiots and the turmoil they constantly created for him.  He decided to begin his free day with a comfortable walk around the city.  He didn't have a destination in mind, but that did not matter.  He was going to savor this forced break from work.  He didn't mind being lost in the big city if it could lead to his also getting lost in thoughts unrelated to his work, his marriage and that idiot Gonzalo.  That's right; it was Adrian Gonzalo who caused all this trouble which led to the current mess in which Canard was being accused of alleged insensitivity and cruelty to a dead animal's stiff and rotting carcass.  "Shit!" he blurted out loud as he remembered he'd left the dead animal in the trunk of his car.  His first reaction to having yelled an expletive aloud on a crowded city street was to slap his hand over his mouth and prepare to apologize to anyone he might have offended.  But it seemed that no one had even noticed his rude utterance.  All the people around him were either engrossed in cell phone conversations, reading newspapers or gossip magazines, wearing earphones or themselves busy shouting even worse obscenities.  The local population was either preoccupied or simply spaced out, but all were definitely uninterested in anyone or anything other than what was going on in their own little world.  Lloyd smiled to himself as he realized that he'd found at least one thing he could like about New York City.

He shortly came upon a park and was content with the idea of sitting for a while.  Out of habit he looked at his watch and saw it was already 12:40 PM.  He was annoyed that he'd even checked the time, but quite happy with the realization that his first day on the PETA assignment was going so well.  He decided just to relax for a bit, even closing his eyes and focusing on the sounds of the birds chirping in the trees and the slowing rhythm of his own breathing.  This was the moment of peace he had hoped for.  He was precipitously yanked back into reality from the sharp pain of a kid rolling his scooter across the toes of his shoe.  He could hear the snickering laughter of a group of kids nearby, so he doubted it had been an accident.  He tried giving the kids a stern look of anger hoping that it would drive them away.  But this gang of city kids just stared back with looks so nasty that they were obviously daring him to challenge them.  Lloyd thought better of it and quickly broke eye contact.  He figured the assault was intentional and meant to draw him into an altercation with the bored youths, so he decided it was best to simply ignore them rather than getting upset and falling into their trap.

Lloyd glanced down at the watch on his wrist. He had told himself he wouldn't be worried about the time, but the habit seemed to be ingrained after years of watching the clock and usually wishing time would pass much faster. It was now almost 2:00 PM. He had to admit that he felt much better now mentally, but sensed a little hunger. He was catching an occasional whiff of freshly grilled hotdogs on the light breeze. Across the park, he could see a man slowly pushing a bright yellow cart with red and green writing labeled 'Guillermo's Dogs & Chorizos.' It was one of those quaint mobile hotdog vending carts, complete with a large red and white umbrella. He thought it a perfect idea to grab a couple of dogs and head back to the hotel. He purchased two hotdogs with light chili and a little mustard as well as a large cup of lemonade. Realizing he had more than he could carry, he wrapped one of the dogs in several napkins before slipping it into the pocket of his sports jacket. Lemonade and dog in hand, he walked back towards the hotel at a leisurely pace while enjoying his improvised picnic lunch.

* * * *

As Lloyd was puttering about and enjoying his time away from that crazy complex, new developments were under way at the Bitewoody Center in Fort Lauderdale. Inspired by the unexpected absence of his boss, Russell Brittle took the initiative to institute a new regime. Feeling the throttle in his hand, Brittle quickly implemented several of the changes he'd previously suggested, but that Chief Canard had been dragging his feet on. The new mandatory physical training program made a huge impact on its very first day. After surprising the days shift officers with orders to stretch, jump, squat, lift, push and run, four officers quit on the spot and two others were injured and placed on workers compensation; one with a twisted ankle and another suffering from a lower back strain. After the rapid loss of six officers, Vice President Webster was forced to take a stand. While he usually preferred to manage from afar and not interfere directly, the fact that the day shift was left precariously undermanned forced him to step in and put a halt to Brittle's tortuous experiment. The

Assistant Chief of course failed to realize his error by jumping into a full-fledged fitness routine with a bunch of men and women who had never even heard of some to the exercises he put them through. Rather than feeling at fault or accepting any blame, Brittle simply explained it to Mr. Webster as, "These people are just so out of shape and completely under motivated that they cannot perform even the simplest workout!"

Webster was concerned about losing control, and eventually having to answer to a higher authority, so he asked, "Is Chief Canard aware of this intense exercise program you've instated?"

"Yes sir" Brittle responded affirmatively. "It's been in the planning stage for several months." While not completely untrue, Brittle's answer was factually inaccurate. The Assistant Chief intentionally misled Webster with this comment, which stretched the real truth that Canard had left Russ's proposal sitting on his desk for months in hopes that Brittle would forget the ridiculous idea. But a mere partial truth was good enough for Brittle who had no qualms about blaming the man he saw as his only obstacle to becoming head of Bitewoody security and whose days he expected were numbered after recent high-profile incidents. Though he tried not to show it, Brittle was ecstatic regarding Chief Canard's recent embarrassing misfortunes and even more filled with glee about his boss's unannounced absence from the center.

Short on staffing, Brittle was glad when Adrian Gonzalo showed up looking for his old job back. Russ even made up for it by promoting him on the spot. Besides, he was planning for the future and building an empire where he was surrounded by loyal, or at least indebted, staff was all part of his master plan. Overall life was good for Brittle and he had every expectation that it would get much better. In Canard's absence he was using his boss's office, drinking his coffee and flirting with his intern. Russ was quite comfortable in the new Acting Chief position he had assumed and was prepared to clean things up around B.E.O.T.CH. To begin with, he got rid of the stained, crusty t-shirt he found underneath Chief Canard's desk. The white streaks of an unknown dried substance on the sides of the trash can only added to the foul images forcing their way into his mind. Russell cringed in disgust as he realized these clues seemed to confirm one of the more recent rumors about Chief Canard's distasteful personal activity making its way among staff.

* * * *

On the home front things were also happening. Perla was beginning to ponder the possible whereabouts of her husband. Of course her imagination began to work overtime to develop a plethora of scenarios of what that horrible, philandering man must be up to. She contacted neighbors to ask for help as well as spread the slanderous accusations about her husband's supposed infidelities. Since she had no knowledge of her husband actually having any friends, she contacted his place of work. Upon reaching the screechy-voiced Elizabeth Jordan, Perla's wild imagination was fueled even more by the young intern's passionate misunderstanding and creative combination of details about Chief Canard's indiscreet onanism, the alleged attack on the female cashier and his mistreatment of the feline that he had so uncaringly and publicly thrown into his car before disappearing. Perla Canard was born and grew up in Belize, so English was not her native language. While she was capable of effective basic communication with most people, the fast talking young Liz's largely indecipherable explanation led to much greater confusion. The already agitated wife was able to pick up just enough words from the conversation to encourage her actively puzzling mind to fill in the gaps with an understanding of the way the world worked based on the many hours of soap operas she had consumed. She ended the telephone call with a mix of feelings. She was quite naturally angry at her husband for having an affair but she was also experiencing an odd sensation of contentment. Her ire was battling her outright satisfaction of finally having evidence and witnesses to prove that her husband had been cheating all along despite his constant denials. Now she only needed to track down her husband so she could really make him pay. She supposed that since no one at Bitewoody seemed to have a clue where he had run off to, then she must enlist the aid of experts in tracking down her husband. Perla figured the police would round up her wayward husband in no time since she'd already uncovered the first big clue: Lloyd's mistress was some woman named 'Felynn.'

Of course Andi Canard had completely forgotten to give her father's message to her mother. Video games, television shows and high school gossip took precedent in the teenager's mind. Even the oddity of her father's absence didn't catch Andi's attention or register any recollection of the distracted phone call she'd received the day before. All of this new information combined with the lack of proper information and multiplied by Perla's overall misunderstanding of reality, meant quite an extraordinary equation was brewing. Perla would eventually relay a preposterous tale to neighbors and the police.

* * * *

Lloyd entered the revolving door of the hotel entrance and dropped his empty cup and soiled napkin into a nearby trash can. As he walked across the lobby the sound of applause perked his curiosity so he glanced into the conference room and realized a new speaker had just been introduced. Seeing as this session was just about to begin, he sauntered in and took a seat along with the rest of the crowd. He didn't think it would hurt to sit in on one short presentation before calling it a day. He was wrong. As usual he underestimated his ability to cause overwhelming havoc with nothing more than his mere presence.

After twenty minutes of trying not to listen to the speaker's explanation of, "Why it's okay to beat your kids, but not your pets," he was eager to leave. He now wondered to himself why he had ventured back in here. He could have stayed a little longer with the delinquents in the park or just returned directly to his hotel room. He guessed that he'd simply became so relaxed that he let his guard down and made a stupid decision. It was too late to do anything about it now. He was stuck until the next break in the program. He tried with all his might to ignore the bile the speaker was flinging out to the eager audience. This obviously angry woman was dressed in baggy men's clothing, wore a strikingly unisex (and very probably self-administered) bowl style haircut and didn't seem anywhere near finished with her diatribe. Oh boy. Lloyd squirmed in his seat and reached into his pockets searching for a pen, paperclip, coin or just anything to occupy his restless hands. He found instead the second hotdog. Well, he had time to pass anyway, so why not finish his lunch? He unrolled the napkins from the now cold dog and quietly began to enjoy his snack. He was completely unaware that his actions were drawing undesired attention. As he slowly chewed on the hotdog he closed his eyes again and tried to imagine he was back in the park. After only two bites of the cylindrical sandwich, he realized there was a growing amount of whispering in the rows of seats directly behind him. He felt the harder-than-friendly tap on his shoulder which was followed by the loudly whispered, "What do you think you are doing?!"

"Huh?" was Lloyd's surprised response, sure that this outburst was not directed at him.

"How could you bring that in here?" the angry woman behind him demanded to know.

"Oh," he asked innocently, "are we not allowed to eat in here?"

"It's not *where* you're eating but *who* you're eating!" corrected the woman who's head Lloyd now noticed was much too large for her glasses.

"Who?" he replied, then uttered, "It's just a hotdog." He had actually been so successful in his attempt to zone out that he had forgotten that he was in the midst of a very intense group of animal lovers, so he was completely caught off guard by the woman's accusation.

"Yes!" she now exclaimed in a raised voice, "you have the blood of our brethren on your lips!"

Before he could catch himself, Lloyd instinctively wiped his mouth with his sleeve, adding the appearance of guilt to his existing perplexed expression.

"Ma'am, it's just my lunch. I didn't kill it; I only bought it from the vendor down the street" he stupidly tried to explain.

"Sir" she responded in an overly sarcastic tone "supporting the trade of murder makes you as culpable as the man wielding the mallet."

Now she was just being ridiculous. The literal translation of what she had just said painted such a silly picture in Canard's mind that he responded with a slim grin. He assumed from her mirthful comment that the woman was only playing a joke on him. He countered with his own humorous response, "Actually it was a woman and it took her half the day to take out that sixteen hundred pound cow with a hammer." Sadly, but not surprisingly, the large animal lover didn't share his sense of humor. Without warning the ample woman jumped up and swiped the hotdog out of his hand. Surprisingly agile for her size, she turned while bouncing up and down in triumph and shouted towards the crowd "We have a murderer among us and he even dares feed upon innocent flesh in our presence!!!"

Lloyd's natural reaction was to attempt to retrieve his lunch. He leaned forward to reach over the row of chairs and grab his hotdog that the woman clenched to her rotund bosom like some kind of bald-headed Barbie doll dressed in a thick, full length coat. As he tried to stretch far enough across the row of seats to reach it, he caught his foot in one of the metal folding chairs. The momentum of his forward reaching motion combined with the loss of balance resulted in his lunging forward with much greater force than intended. As he teetered there momentarily his body tensed causing his outstretched hand to clench tightly as he prepared for the expected fall to the floor. Unfortunately his momentum carried him forward and his outstretched fist landed squarely on the uppermost chin of the dog swiping cow defender. Of course, the highlight of Lloyd's little lurching dance occurred just as the attention of everyone in the hall was turning to look towards the screaming lady. All eyes were on him just as his fist flew up and made solid contact with the woman's face. The oversized lunch snarfer was relieved of her undersized glasses and immediately rendered unconscious. She flopped down hard on the floor in full compliance with Newton's law of gravity. Lloyd too fell down, but quickly sprung back to his feet in response to the manly-looking woman on stage screaming at the top of her lungs: "Get Him!!!"

The crowd surged on demand and moved towards the rear of the hall as he desperately scrambled through the mess of strewn chairs and went fleeing for the door. He ran as hard as he could, heart pounding in his chest, out of the hall, through the lobby, out the front door and down the sidewalk in the same direction which he had strolled so casually only a few hours earlier. The mob surged onto the sidewalk and roared loudly in pursuit as they tossed loud, angry, anti-carnivorous slogans and slurs behind the fleeing flesh feeder. Lloyd could hear shouts of "murderer" and "flesh eater" being hurled behind him, but he dared not look back. Most stunning was hearing the label "you animal" cast as an insult. It struck him as oddly ironic that the PETA crowd would choose to use this term as an insult, when logically this label should have caused them to treat him with the great compassion they claimed to have for all lesser critters.

Finally feeling comfortable that the mob wasn't still following, he slowed to an easier pace. Heaving to catch his breath, Lloyd felt thankful that none of the women in attendance were lighter than two hundred fifty pounds. Exhaling strongly, he raised his brow in quiet contemplation at how all those animal-loving, meat-loathing women could have put on so much weight from a meat-free, animal-friendly diet. Maybe if they had to cultivate or forage their own greens they might actually look more the part. But that was always the way with these people; put on a show, talk out of the side of your mouth, but live your life in the manner you wished regardless of the overwhelmingly obvious hypocrisy. For the first time it struck him that he had noticed only women in the conference hall. Though he hadn't really been looking much at people he was almost sure. To be honest, it was a bit hard to determine at a mere glance as most of these ladies' girth prevented the detection of any specifically definitive female anatomy. Not to mention that most sported manly short style haircuts, were dressed in pants and wore either sneakers or flat leather sandals showing off their dry, scaly, unkempt feet.

"Whew!" Lloyd panted loudly. He'd worked up a quite a lather in his escape. He lifted his arm to wipe his dripping forehead on his sleeve then let out a grunt of pain, "Ouch!" He had poked himself in the eye with the remaining half of the hotdog. He had not even realized until then that he had successfully removed it from that nasty woman's sweaty, heaving bosom. Oh well, he wouldn't eat it now anyway, even if he had still been hungry. He tossed it into the next trash can he passed on the street. He thrust his hands deep in his pockets, sighed heavily and shook his lowered head at the weird sort of people he seemed to always attract wherever he ventured. Lloyd continued walking without much of a plan except that he was pretty sure that returning to the hotel anytime soon would be a very big mistake.

* * * *

Fort Lauderdale-Hollywood Airport maintenance and security personnel had traced the horrible stench to Canard's car. Sure that such an awful smell had to indicate foul play; they made the quick decision to call in the police to check out the obnoxiously odorous vehicle. So certain that the trunk contained a human corpse, airport officials reported it as having found a dead body. Fort Lauderdale Police Detective Abel Fleenor jumped at the chance to respond to that call. His motivation was more tied to personal aspirations than actual crime solving. The recognition sure to follow a high-profile murder case at the international airport was just what he needed to make a name for himself and jumpstart his lagging career.

By the time Fleenor had arrived on the scene word had spread throughout the airport's employees as well as the local media. There was quite a crowd gathered to witness the detective's flamboyant breeching of the suspicious vehicle's trunk. The excitement was extinguished quickly when it was determined that the true victim was a cat. Fleenor was disgusted by the smell and appalled that his expertise had been wasted on the handling of a weeklong dead cat. But still determined to do his job to the best of his ability, Abel proceeded to take note of the police-style equipment belt and handheld radio accompanying the body, as well as the identification badge of one 'Adrian Gonzalo.' Fleenor had the plates and VIN number run through police dispatch and came up with a clean registration to a Lloyd Canard. He documented the incident as well as all of his actions, but that was the extent of what he would do since it was really nothing more than a dead cat. Everything went in his report and he worked rapidly so he could depart the smelly scene as quickly as possible. Nothing quite compares to the horribly foul stench of a rapidly decomposing cat carcass in the blistering South Florida heat. But even that didn't quell the crowd of curious observers who had been attracted to the scene as buzzards to road kill. That this awful smell actually *was* road kill was simply coincidental.

Detective Fleenor overheard some of the more extravagantly liberal onlookers discussing the fact that the officer had not yet dusted the cat for fingerprints. They seemed to be under the impression that having left a dead cat in the trunk of a car at the Fort Lauderdale Airport must certainly somehow be classified as a felony. As the crowd became more worked up a few onlookers began raising verbal protests. They were insistent that the police treat the corpse with dignity, dust the feline's fur for fingerprints, deliver the body to the medical examiner and attempt to ascertain the cause of death and bring the murderer to justice. Detective Fleenor did not respond to the taunts, but simply turned from the crowd and shook his head in amazement at the wild ideas these people conjured. Didn't they have jobs or homes to go to? Who hung out at the airport if they weren't on their way to or from somewhere? Were their lives so completely perfect that they had nothing better to occupy their time?

Airport personnel were hopeful that the police would remove the vehicle, but Detective Fleenor explained that there was no reason for him to legally do so. Someone suggested that the concept of a public nuisance be employed. Fleenor certainly agreed with their determination that this awful smell was in fact a disturbance of the peace, but explained that he had no authority to drag the vehicle to police impound based on that alone. He offered the suggestion that the airport utilize their own security incident reports along with his police report to remove the stinky automobile from airport premises at the expense of the obviously irresponsible owner.

After being made to look like a fool at the airport, Detective Fleenor decided to take a break and stop for a cup of coffee. He even turned off his radio to escape the annoying meowing sounds that his recent activity had stirred up among his less-than-professional coworkers. Cops could be an exceedingly difficult bunch to deal with. Most had strong personalities, were highly competitive as well as extremely unforgiving. They were not lenient at all with the mistakes or misfortunes of fellow officers. When the chance came along to tear down one of their peers the majority of them would jump on the opportunity with vigor not unlike that of a bunch of middle school aged children. Fleenor felt used, abused, totally under challenged and absolutely unappreciated in this job. Abel walked into the diner with his head hung low and chose a corner table away from other customers as he really wanted to be alone with his thoughts and to deeply contemplate his career. Abel Fleenor was a middle-aged Fort Lauderdale Police Detective who wore the facial creases of a much older man. Despite this most recent embarrassment to his ego, Abel's confidence was not diminished. He just knew that he was capable of excelling in this line of work. All he needed was the opportunity to show everyone that he really could handle a big, important case. When the waitress came by he told her, "Black coffee and a regular donut please." He then removed his glasses and rubbed his forehead in a fruitless effort to wipe away all the bad thoughts.

Fleenor had always felt himself pulled towards a career in public service. He was raised by a civil servant father and taught to believe in the importance of pride and a strong support of one's country and citizenry from an early age. As in the case of most young boys, Abel longed to follow in his father's footsteps. But as he grew older he was able to see the disparity between the ideals his father preached and the reality in which he actually lived. He witnessed the slow demise of his father's pride as he had his dreams dismantled one day at a time over the course of a career spanning nearly three decades. It is always a sad thing to see a proud man eventually broken under the strain of rampantly aggressive stupidity. It is doubly so when this man is your father. By the time Abel reached manhood, his father had finally begun to open up about the details of his disappointing career. His father shared stories of the small minded, long winded supervisors with an aggressively malicious management style who rewarded only their most favored subordinates and endlessly harassed those whom they disliked for petty, subjective reasons. These imperious managers exhibited subverted feelings of superiority in an agency with little lateral opportunity and no chance to develop skills useful in other fields or transfer to a more competent and critical agencies. It was the old man's dire, explicit warnings combined with the clear evidence of his experiences with hateful, vindictive supervisors that really scared Fleenor away from following his father's path into federal law enforcement.

Abel's frustrations led him to the idea that if his coworkers and department were going to treat him like one of the crappy employees who'd long since given up on a glorious crime fighting career, then he might as well resign himself to behave exactly like that. At least that's how he consoled himself as the waitress delivered his badly needed dosage of caffeine and sugar. As he washed the sweet glazed treat down his throat with the bitter, hot liquid he had a vision of himself sitting in the same spot twenty years from now. The image he conjured of his future self sitting alone in the coffee shop, was prematurely bald, wore the permanent scowl of a curmudgeonly cynic and carried an extra forty pounds around his waist. Fleenor didn't like that vision at all. There was no way he could quit after witnessing his own fathers dogged persistence in the face of even greater adversity. His fellow police officers could waste their time making cat noises over the radio, but Abel was determined not to give up so easily. He felt he still had sufficient time and talent to vindicate both himself and his father. Detective Fleenor dropped what remained of the donut onto the plate, took one more swig of coffee to wash it all down his throat, replaced the glasses on his face, slapped four one dollar bills on the table and sprinted out to the parking lot. On his way back to his car, Abel clicked his handheld radio back on just in time to hear a call coming in for him. He didn't know if it was the first attempt dispatch had made to reach him but he responded boldly and without apology. He had a job to do and some fabulous professional potential to salvage.

When the call came in for him to respond to a missing persons report, Fleenor realized immediately that it was a joke meant to belittle him. Wives reporting missing husbands were common occurrences and these calls almost always ended up being complete wastes of time and police resources. But as public servants they could not simply ignore such a call, so the assignment was usually pushed off on rookies or officers considered incapable of handling more crucial police business. Today, Fleenor fell into that category.

A missing persons run. It was a blatant slap in the face to dispatch a seasoned officer like him on this sore consolation prize. Abel's best hope was that the wife reporting the missing spouse might have actually murdered the sod so he could actually do some real productive police work. Fleenor was only slightly troubled at the realization of that morbid thought going through his head, but those are the type things that a lot of cops dream of. Many police officers find the day-to-day job tediously boring. Part of the reason for this can be blamed on having grown up on movies, video games and police television shows in mental preparation for a career filled with the non-stop action of daily shootouts, frequent head-bashing of punks and wildly reckless (yet amazingly wreck-free) vehicle pursuits through crowded city streets.  The real life, day-to-day business of law enforcement left much wanting for these types.

When the detective received the name and address of the allegedly missing person, he paused for a moment.  "Lloyd Canard" Fleenor repeated aloud.  Was this part of someone's elaborate joke or merely a coincidence?  He hadn't submitted his official report on the response to the airport call yet, so it was unlikely anyone else would have easy access to the name of the vehicle's registered owner.  Maybe he'd happen upon something after all.  Since the call to the residence wasn't urgent and he already had a head start on background information by knowing the missing man's car was parked at the airport, Fleenor decided to stop by Canard's place of employment first to see what additional clues he might glean.  Who knows...he might just be able to solve this missing person thing before meeting the wife.  It would certainly be impressive to show up at the house and inform the man's spouse of exactly what the situation was, whether he was cavorting or simply avoiding home.  The result didn't really matter to Fleenor as much as reaching a quick conclusion to what was probably just a domestic argument, which often resulted in the husband leaving the house for several hours or sometimes a few days to cool down before he finally accepted the fact that his life sucks and he's stuck in it with nowhere else to go except back into the lion's den.  And after pushing the lioness to the point of calling the police, the poor sap might as well return home wearing a suit of raw meat.

Detective Fleenor did not yet realize that he was going to really earn his pay today.  He arrived at B.E.O.T.C.H. and identified himself and the subject of his inquiry to the officer on Post One.  Night shift Security Supervisor Earl Markey was just heading out of the building.  Fueled more by curiosity than professional interest, Markey introduced himself to the detective and asked how he might offer his assistance.

Though it wasn't necessarily helpful to the investigation, it did make an interesting start to have Fleenor's first interview commence with details of the lewd act that Lloyd Canard had been so publicly performing just a couple days before his disappearance.

Fleenor also collected an interesting statement from Adrian Gonzalo who had shown up early to prepare for his new supervisory duties by shadowing Mr. Markey.  Gonzalo recalled the smell of stale liquor on Mr. Canard's breath and the blood-shot eyes as he glared at him and fired him on the spot for attempting to save a 'critically injured kitten' as Fleenor's notes quoted Gonzalo. Gonzalo also took this opportunity to try impressing both Markey and Fleenor with his view that "Chief Canard doesn't like me anyway because of my war record and personal involvement with the President."

Both men stared at Gonzalo and then looked at each other. Markey shrugged his shoulders to indicate his bewilderment, so Fleenor felt compelled to inquire. "Would you mind elaborating on what exactly you mean by that?"

"Sure," explained Gonzalo, "I think he feels inferior to me because of information I shared with him about my previous life."

"Go on" prodded Fleenor reluctantly.

Gonzalo proceeded to reveal to these two dumbfounded men that during the Gulf War in 1990, he had been contacted directly by the president of the United States who sought his counsel and advice on exactly how to proceed with the removal of Saddam Hussein from Kuwait. Fleenor barely managed to prevent his jaw hitting the floor with the tale he was hearing. Realizing that this was heading in a direction unrelated to the investigation, and that the man must be off his rocker, Fleenor cut off Gonzalo by interrupting with, "I think you should be careful you don't reveal too much."

"Oh yeah, that's a good point" Gonzalo whispered conspiratorially as he gave the uncomfortable detective a nudge and a wink.

"Well!" exclaimed Fleenor. "I think I've got all the information I need here...and probably a little more." The detective glanced back towards Mr. Markey who responded only with an embarrassed nod of apology for Gonzalo's unhelpful intrusion.

Next, Detective Fleenor met with Miss Jordan. He gladly accepted the cup of coffee Elizabeth offered, and then asked her about anything odd she may have noticed in her boss's recent behavior. Fleenor heard yet another tale of Lloyd's cruelty to an animal in Miss Jordan's mixed up version of the fish bowl he'd attempted to give her. Fleenor had the picture of a poor little fish being brutally caged and displayed as on the gallows to exacerbate the penalty of restricted freedom. Abel was detecting a definite pattern in Lloyd's behavior and the revealing portrait of a madman about to crack and let loose his rage on the world was emerging.

When the questioning turned to extracurricular activities, particularly focusing on the possibility of an extramarital affair, Fleenor noticed an instant change it Miss Jordan's attitude. Though Liz said she had no knowledge of any affair, Abel picked up on signs that she was not being completely truthful. The question caused her posture to stiffen and her eyes immediately averted to the floor. The detective also noticed that her left leg which she had crossed on top of her right began a rhythmically nervous bounce. Fleenor misread the secretary's youthful jealously over the possibility of Mr. Canard having eyes for another woman as Miss Jordan's attempting to cover up for her wayward boss. Fleenor made a mental note that she appeared uneasy, but pursued it no further at this point. It seemed that, detective or not, Abel Fleenor was no better at reading women than the next guy.

The eager detective next ventured into the casino where he asked Giovanni Bigglio about Lloyd's behavior with particular interest focused on gambling, alcohol consumption and the recent incident involving the poor defenseless cashier. Bigglio had already been very concerned about Canard's mysterious, unannounced absence, so the detective's arrival really shook him up. He answered Fleenor's questions truthfully, but refrained from garnishing the tales as most other employees had done. Fleenor noticed Bigglio's reluctance to embellish, but with his consistent lack of instinct Abel mistakenly read the lack of adornment as being uncooperative and cited this in his notes.

Mr. Webster was most surprised at the detective's inquiry.

"Disappeared?" laughed Webster. "Shoot, I sent that sucker out of town after the dead cat incident."

"Out of town?" inquired Fleenor.

"Yes sir. I sent him up to New York City for this three day conference while things calm down here."

When further questioning revealed that Canard was actually sent to a PETA conference focusing on equal rights for all animals, Fleenor directly questioned the judgment of Mr. Webster in light of Lloyd's quite evident aversion to other species. The detective point-blank informed the vice president that he might very well be considered an accessory should Canard follow his previous record of destructive behavior and act out in this particularly volatile pro-animal environment.

"Well...I had no idea" said the flabbergasted Webster. "I never heard those other stories and I thought he was just another regular guy dealing with an unhappy life, unfulfilling career and disappointing marriage. I had no clue that that he suffered some much deeper problems."

"Mr. Webster," Detective Fleenor responded instructively, "haven't you yourself just told me about this disgustingly vicious cat business?"

"Well," Webster began, then hesitated for a moment. "Yes I did, but I had no idea it was premeditated or exhibited some type of aberrant affliction."

"So as punishment for showing an abominable insensitivity towards an injured cat, you decided to send this man to an animal lover's convention?" Fleenor's question placed the pieces together to clearly show the vice president his errors.

Steve Webster swallowed hard and tried to defend himself by whining the security officer's anthem: "But, I didn't know." This new information made Webster sick with worry and concerned more about his own involvement than anything else. It was time to pull a porcupine and extend his quills in self defense. Webster tried to be as helpful as possible to the detective, even offering a copy of the six page complaint from the casino cashier. The extra step he took by suggesting the possibility that there was some connection between the two incidents: "Who knows? It might even have been her cat?" only added further confusion to Fleenor's thoroughly exaggerated profile of an innocent man.

Detective Fleenor asked to see the cashier but was informed that she was out on sick leave. Abel incorrectly assumed it was to recover from injuries sustained in Canard's assault. No one bothered to share the well known fact that the cashier was a raging alcoholic with an established pattern of missing work to recover from her frequent binges.

As Fleenor began the interview with Assistant Chief Brittle he was still hoping to gain a greater insight into the cashier assault and ultimately determine whether there might truly be some connection to other recent events. Since his mind had already turned away from the missing person issue, Abel broached the subject from the angle, "Do you have any information or suspicions connecting Mr. Canard with any acts of violence or involving any animal abuse concerns?  Possibly being specifically related to cats?" he focused.

Not being the brightest bulb in the candle, Brittle misinterpreted that line of questioning to indicate that the detective must be looking into some bestiality allegations.  His demeanor changed very quickly at that assumption.  Detective Fleenor recognized the change in him and naturally suspected that Assistant Chief Brittle was attempting to cover up something relevant he knew about Lloyd Canard's anti-animal activities.  The truth was that while Russ Brittle did become extremely nervous when he mistook the question to indicate that the police were snooping around about bestiality claims, he also felt a new sense of respect for Chief Canard.  It appeared that he had more in common with his boss than he had previously realized.  While Brittle had never attempted feline frottage as he believed the detective seemed to be investigating, he couldn't help but appreciate that Chief Canard apparently shared some of his more preposterously perverse proclivities.  So Brittle played dumb and avoided the subject by ignoring the question completely and instead detailing what he thought were the best abdominal workouts.  Fleenor added a comment on this lack of candor in his notebook and circled the name for a possible follow-up.

Before leaving B.E.O.T.C.H., Detective Fleenor asked to have a look at Chief Canard's office.  Here he found the dead fish floating in the bowl of water.  Certain that he was on to something, Abel dipped out the dead fish, sealed it in a plastic bag and deposited it in his coat pocket as evidence.

Fleenor began to consider that this was more than a mere missing person.  The more he learned of Canard the more he realized that his so-called disappearance was most probably a well-crafted escape planned in advance and set into action by some recent event which served as the trigger.  Fleenor wore a slight smile as he returned to his car and contemplated his next move.  He was highly impressed with the strength of his own inquisitive mind.  The truth was that Fleenor's mind was much less 'inquisitive' than it was 'creative.'  Having significantly less investigative experience than he had in the library and video store with detective stories and dramatic movies, he felt sure that he was on the brink of something huge.  Doubtless breaking open this case would get him noticed and invigorate his stagnant career. So in Abel's exuberant ignorance he continued discounting the facts and instead focused on developing his own fictional scenario of the madman he imagined he was hunting.

On his way out of the Bitewoody Center, Fleenor stopped in the lobby restroom. Gonzalo, feeling he'd made a connection with the investigator and hoping it might evolve into a new career opportunity, followed the detective into the men's room. It wasn't that he was unsatisfied with his new position, but he was concerned that his rehiring and promotion might not survive Chief Canard's return. Gonzalo eagerly placed himself in front of the urinal right next to Detective Fleenor and continued offering his unsolicited and highly questionable resume. Fleenor quickly finished up and scampered across to the row of sinks. Gonzalo was right at his elbow. Fleenor washed his hands then hit the button on the hand dryer. He stood closer than necessary to prevent Gonzalo from coming in beside him and hoped this would aid his escape from this parasitic nut-job by making him wait to dry his hands. Gonzalo didn't miss a beat as he quickly snatched a toilet seat cover out of the dispenser on the wall to dry his hands. Fleenor was not sure how anyone could dry their hands with that slick wax paper, but he put it down to eccentricity and headed quickly for the exit and the refuge of his car.

Detective Fleenor had collected quite a bit of information from this visit to the Bitewoody Center and realized that he had a great deal of work to do. With his notebook full of fancifully fictitious facts and a head swarming with marvelous dreams of groundless grandeur, Fleenor hopped into his car and headed towards the Canard residence.

* * * *

The animal-loving, vegetarian crowd seethed with anger over the hotdog incident. Their disgust with the meat-eating interloper would have passed quickly, but it was his striking of a woman and escape from their wrath which infuriated them most. After reconvening in the conference room, someone noticed the bleeding beef defender still lying on the floor unattended. At this point they briefly looked around the room...each hoping quietly that someone else would go to her aid. Reluctantly a few of them in the front of the crowd cleared the fallen chairs and began attending to her. Actually they just sort of called out and poked at her as they were much less enthusiastic about helping one of their own than they were some fictive feral animal. They shouted for someone near the door to ask the hotel desk attendant to call for a doctor. Word was passed inefficiently through the crowd and one of the excited round women finally spoke with the hotel clerk. Instead of simply requesting an ambulance, the fast talking, wound up Puerto Rican woman attempted to explain in detail what had occurred. Her rapid, convoluted rant included irrelevant details about, "dis poor animal," and excessive usage of the emphatic expression, "ju know wha ay mean?"

The speedy, incoherent speech left the clerk completely confused and he entirely misunderstood what the Boricua lady intended to be a request for medical assistance. The injured woman eventually regained consciousness and was able to sit up and take a little water. The onlookers encouraged her to remain as still as possible until she could be evaluated by medical personnel. The PETA members who had not yet abandoned the scene by slinking off to their rooms to consume carefully concealed caches of chocolates and chips by Nestle and Frito-Lay were quite relieved to finally feel that they may soon be able to get out of there as well.

Someone wondered aloud just what was taking the ambulance so long to arrive. Nearly forty minutes had passed since the incident and more than thirty since someone must have notified the paramedics. One of the more concerned members approached the front desk to inquire as to the delay in arrival of medical treatment. The clerk seemed a bit perturbed as he explained that he had made several phone calls but never found a veterinarian that would make a house call. This confusion soon exploded into more outraged PETA attendees bombarding the lobby and aggressively protesting the clerk's disrespectful attitude. Hotel security became involved and the collection of statements they received seemed to indicate that some animal-hating terrorist had thwarted security, invaded the conference hall and ultimately attacked an innocent lady while wielding a dead animal in his hand then proceeded to further put the poor woman at risk by somehow intervening with the timely notification of emergency medical personnel.  This evolving ruckus was becoming too much for hotel security to handle alone and the clerk dialed 911.

* * * *

With no plan of where to go and no hope for returning to the hotel until much later, Lloyd wandered the streets until he reached the same park he'd visited earlier in the day.  He happily noticed that the teen skater hooligans were nowhere in sight.  He took a seat in the shade of a large sycamore where he expected to rest for a bit while considering his next possible move.  Becoming more comfortable, he leaned back against the tree.  He relaxed by watching an elderly gentleman toss seeds to a noisy flock of excited pigeons before slowly dozing off right there in the park.

* * * *

It was a newly invigorated Fleenor that arrived in front of the Canard residence twenty minutes after leaving Bitewoody.  He was determined to ensure that the new spring in his step was a result of motivation for the job and not simply a side effect of the sugar and caffeine he had so recently ingested.

A very excited Perla Canard met the detective at the door. He politely introduced himself and asked the distraught woman to settle down.  They both sat on the sofa and Fleenor began his questioning slowly in an effort to put her at ease.  After commencing with the basic biological data such as name and description, Abel eased toward extracurricular activities like hobbies, interests, clubs and any close associates.  With the emotional woman finally calmed, Fleenor was ready to pursue information more relevant to his investigation.  He delicately inquired about any pets the couple might have as he was still not yet sure of the origin of the deceased animal found in Canard's car.

The detective was suddenly shaken by a massive repositioning from deep within his intestines.  He had no desire to interrupt the interview, but almost immediately he could tell that this particular disruption would not be something he could put on hold.  His blatantly unbinding bowels beat out his preferred professionalism as he realized this matter could not possibly wait. He came shakily onto his feet but was unable to stand up straight.

He remained bent at the waist like President Obama greeting the Mayor of Tampa. With one hand grasping his irreverently gurgling guts, he could only manage to blurt out a single strained word to get the point across: "Bathroom!"

Perla was shocked at the detective's actions, but could see from his bulging eyes, clenched teeth and poor posture that he was in extreme discomfort from the pressure of an uncontrollable movement. Abel struggled to waddle from the living room down the hallway to the bathroom where Perla led him. He barely made it before the dam burst and the flood gushed loose. Fleenor groaned in agony as he pondered what he had consumed that disagreed so horribly with his system. Painful as it was the entire process was over in a curt cataclysmic cascade. He sat for another moment to regain his composure then stood up to finish. Once he had cleaned up and had his pants back on he reached to flush the toilet. The plumbing did not respond. Abel jiggled the handle several times, but nothing happened. He started getting nervous as he lifted the cover and checked the internal mechanisms, but he couldn't make it work. That was the extent of the detective's plumbing ability, but he lingered in the bathroom a little longer trying to figure out what to do. Alarmed and embarrassed he had to finally clean up, put on a brave face and depart the room without disposing of the waste. Fleenor embarrassingly informed Mrs. Canard that there appeared to be a problem with the toilet. Perla nonchalantly explained that she had been forced to turn off the water to prevent her husband from flushing prior to her inspection. Fleenor didn't know what to think or say as he'd never heard anything so odd.

With that calamity behind him, or in fact floating in the room next door, Fleenor pulled himself together and resumed the interview with Mrs. Canard in the dining room. He asked the lady to describe in detail the days preceding her husband's disappearance. What Perla Canard relayed to Detective Fleenor was both absolutely wrong and very imaginatively created. She portrayed herself as the forsaken wife, abused by an overbearing and cold-hearted husband. She told the perplexed investigator, "An now I know the udder woman name ez Felynn," as she put into play all of the excessively emotional scenes she had collected in her mind over the years of watching soap operas. She cried on demand, thrashed about violently, staring and screaming off into the empty corner of the room where she imagined the cameras would be positioned, before finally throwing herself into the arms of Detective Fleenor with all the vigor of a hyperactive juvenile. Unfortunately, Fleenor was busy taking notes and trying to take quick glances toward the empty corner of the room where Perla kept averting her eyes. It was in one of these instances that she tossed herself towards him, but ended up on the floor at his feet. Fleenor jumped in surprise, then stared down at the even more surprised Perla and delivered an unapologetic, "Sorry," before returning to his notebook. Perla felt a rush of embarrassment to be working with so incapable a man. Not once had she ever seen them miss that cue on television and they certainly had never allowed the star of the performance to drop onto the dining room floor.

Formalities finished, Fleenor apologized again for having left the mess in the bathroom, though he was now aware that he actually had no fault in the failed flusher.

Perla said "Ez no problem, I'll have a look en just one minute."

"I wish you didn't have to," he offered again, "it's just that I must have eaten something that didn't agree with me."

"Not to worry," Perla sang, "I tell you what wrong in one minute."

Perla popped into the bathroom and returned a moment later to announce her diagnosis: "You eat something not so good."

"Yes, I have to agree with that" responded Fleenor.

"Now you know" reiterated the wannabe doctor with a penchant to always have the last word.

'Now I know quite a few things' Fleenor thought, as he sensed that queasy feeling all over again from her overly intense interest in his watery waste. Abel did wonder what had upset his stomach so. Maybe he'd been served a bad donut. He just hoped he wasn't coming down with anything serious.

Fleenor soon departed the house with a photograph of Lloyd and a notebook full of his exploits as imagined by Perla. Driving away, he radioed dispatch to confirm his completion of the call and resumed availability. In his rearview mirror he spotted the crumpled figure of Perla Canard now well into the throes of performing 'act two' on her front lawn. He pretended not to notice as he turned in the direction of the Fort Lauderdale Airport.

* * * *

Lloyd snapped awake as he jumped in his sleep from some unremembered dream. For half a second he was bewildered and completely confused by his surroundings. Remembering where he was and why he was hiding out in the park, Lloyd looked down at his watch. "Shit!" he exclaimed more loudly than he'd intended, but with spot on literal accuracy. The pigeons had evidently digested their bird seed and then proceeded to relieve themselves while perched on a limb directly above his head.

"Of course" he said out loud, not surprised in the least by his latest misfortune.

* * * *

Barbara was one of the coordinators of the PETA conference and one of the ladies who took the attack in the assembly most seriously. She checked the roster of registration attendees, and since male participants were few, was able to quickly identify the problem maker as a Mr. Lloyd Canard. She then proceeded to the front desk and asked the clerk if she could confirm the room number of a friend. The clerk lifted the phone and said, "I'll give him a call and let him know you are looking for him."

"Oh no!" the conniving woman interrupted, "he said he would be napping after the conference and I'm not supposed to wake him until later for dinner."

"Oh, alright" the clerk responded while quickly replacing the receiver on the cradle. "Mr. Canard is in room 1228."

Barbara quickly assembled a small group of large women to accompany her on a clandestine mission to the twelfth floor. They made a mess of his room, emptied his duffel bag, ripped his clothing and just for good measure soaked all the pieces in the toilet and bathtub. The only bright side for Lloyd was that he had traveled on short notice and brought along very little clothing or personal property. This fact only seemed to further enrage the PETA extremists and they made quick work of completely destroying the room. They were neither quiet nor discreet during this process, so another guest overheard the ruckus and reported the egregious vandalism to hotel personnel. Hotel security was dispatched, but the small team of oversized aggressors had dispersed before the officers arrived on the scene. All that was left for them to do was document the results of the ruinous raid and begin the search for the individual who was registered in this room.

* * * *

Driving away from the Canard home, Detective Fleenor had dispatch contact the Fort Lauderdale Airport authorities to determine where Mr. Canard's vehicle had been towed. As additional facts had come to light, Abel felt it would be a good idea to perform a thorough search of the abandoned vehicle.

The cat carcass had not been removed in accordance with a strict policy of the towing company regarding property found in vehicles. The parked car seemed even smellier now that Abel had no other noses around to help consume the stinky fumes. He found no clues, but cut his visit short after having retched twice. Overwhelmed by the reeking scent permeating his suit, he returned directly to the station for a shower and change of clothes. On his way home Abel stopped by the dry cleaner to drop off his shirt, slacks and jacket.

* * * *

Lloyd soon found that his attempts to remove the fresh white poop from his shoulders and lapel only smeared the feces around and ground it deeper into the fabric of his sports jacket. Giving up in frustration he finally looked to see who might be watching and laughing at him. He didn't see anyone looking in his direction. That was a rare reprieve from well-deserved embarrassment. In fact, he now saw that all attention was focused on a small cluster of people formed in a circle across the park. He checked his watch. He wanted to return to his hotel to change, shower, relax and maybe actually enjoy some of his break away from the Bitewoody complex. He figured the longer he waited to show his face back at the hotel again, the safer his return might be.

The sound of laughter called his attention once again to the crowd of people at the edge of the park. Curious, he walked over and peeked into the circle. There was a mime in the center of the group quietly performing a silent show. He was unimpressed with what he observed as a ridiculous art and totally useless talent. He wanted to walk away but felt compelled to remain a while longer so as not to appear rude and elicit unwanted attention to himself. He should have known that such a result was unavoidable for a fate marked man like himself.

The chalky-faced mime performed silently and didn't seem to concern the nearly tame pigeons pecking around for crumbs. One of the passersby had a dog on a lead. The canine's curious sniffing finally disturbed one of the pigeons and it flew up into the air. As birds usually do, the flock followed. Lloyd flinched, lifting his arm to shield himself from the noisy gray cloud rising too close to his head. His arm only barely clipped the pigeon, but the overweight bird squawked in surprise and drew the full attention of the crowd. The full-bellied pigeon fluttered fitfully under its own weight and shed a small cloud of feathers that lightly hung in the air just long enough to exaggerate the force of actual impact. Lloyd couldn't help but think of the similarities between this pigeon's performance and the overdramatic reactions often exhibited by his wife. The humorous resemblance brought a rare smile to Canard's face. Regrettably, that smile was very ill timed. The crowd rippled with surprise. The mime froze: but only momentarily. This was too much for the performer of still undetermined gender to take. It peeled the small black beret from its head and tossed it to the ground. Lloyd thought the mime was upset that the pigeon had drawn attention away from the act, but he soon learned better when the mime marched towards him determinedly. He thought he saw the mime trembling, but was more drawn into the fiercely squinted eyes that were locked on him. The mime spoke: "You tourists come here and just think you can do anything you please! Treating the local people and environment in any manner you wish and exhibiting all sorts of rude, anti-social behavior."

The crowd gasped. Lloyd took a step back. The squinting, bloodshot eyes contrasted frighteningly with the pale face as the mime screamed, "How dare you come in here and mistreat these poor animals that are forced to hunt for scraps of food simply to survive! They used to live free and reign strong in this country until your kind of people moved in, cut down the trees and paved everything with concrete. I want you to get out of my sight, out of my park and out of my city!"

Most of the crowd was still stunned, but some were beginning to shake their heads in agreement with the mime. Applause slowly rose from the congregation as they began to mumble to each other and point at Lloyd. Lloyd knew from recent experience just how volatile an emotional crowd could be. Especially when motivated by some perceived danger or cruelty to animals. Now was not the time to try to explain that the fat pigeon was clearly not starving and that the bird was frightened by the dog and actually flew into his hand rather than the other way around. Instinctively he said nothing as he cautiously backed away three or four steps, then turned and walked away briskly. He tilted his head slightly and listened closely for the sound of an advancing crowd. Thankfully this lot didn't pursue him.

Lloyd looked at the time and decided he would chance venturing towards the hotel. He could observe from afar before approaching just to be sure, but he hoped things had calmed down and the angry overweight women had ended their conference for the day and moved on to enjoy their large vegetarian dinners. He couldn't keep the little smile off his face when the picture of all those large, butch women seated behind tiny bowls of salad formed in his mind. He knew it was an unlikely scenario, but their blatant hypocrisy was simply hilarious.

He observed the front of the hotel from across the street for fifteen minutes before working up the nerve to approach the door. When he entered the lobby, Lloyd found the conference finished for the day and the area almost completely vacant of guests. The few who were there paid him no attention at all so he moved straight to the front desk. He presented his driver's license and whispered to the clerk, "I'm sorry, but I've misplaced my room key. May I have another copy please?"

The clerk read the name on the license and checked the reservations database. The observant clerk then made a quick double-take, locked stares with Lloyd for a second then quickly averted his eyes back down to the computer monitor. He noticed the action, but since the clerk didn't say anything he hoped it was nothing more than the employee being thorough in attempting to confirm his identity. At least that's how he tried to console himself. The clerk handed the key card across the counter without looking directly at him again. Lloyd accepted the key, said a quick, "Thank you," and then headed down the hallway. As he entered the empty elevator, the clerk picked up his radio and said only: "The guest from 1228 is on his way up."

He kept his head down on the ride up. It had been a long day and he was feeling very drained. When the elevator doors slid open, he was already a full step out when he lifted his head and saw two men directly in his path. One was a short, slightly pudgy gentleman in a brown suit, white shirt and bright paisley tie holding a handheld radio. The other man was tall, thin, wearing a dark blue police uniform, holding a clipboard in his left hand while his right hand rested on the butt of the pistol anchored to his right hip. Lloyd stopped dead in his tracks, exhaled strongly and dropped his shoulders in surrender. The uniformed policeman spoke in an uncharacteristically high-pitched voice for such a large man, "Mr. Lloyd Canard?"

"Yes sir" he admitted.

The officer began bombarding Lloyd with questions which seemed to be coming from deep out of left field. He had no idea about the vandalism of hotel property or any rowdy roommates. He tried to explain that he had been out of the hotel room the entire day and had no idea who might have entered his room nor why. The officer's looked him up and down then looked at each other before the shorter one asked, "Are you sure you haven't been sleeping in the street?"

Lloyd forced an insincere smile at what he knew was a shot at his appearance with bird turd and feathers stuck to his jacket. "I fell asleep in the park and the pigeons had a go at me" was all he offered.

"Can you show us some identification please?" the taller officer requested. Although phrased as a question, Lloyd understood it was an order with which he had no choice but to comply. He produced his driver's license. Convinced they had the right guy, the officers commenced more direct questioning of the disheveled suspect. Albeit still confused, Lloyd was actually quite comforted that he was being queried regarding something which he hadn't been a part of for a change. This didn't last long. Officer Garland, as his name plate indicated, calmly asked, "Mr. Canard, do you recall whether your departure from the hotel occurred before or after the assault in the conference hall?"

"Well of course it was after the accident." Then added, "but I don't think it should be classified as an assault officer."

"You don't do you?" Officer Garland inquired with raised eyebrows. "Exactly how would you classify what took place Mr. Canard?"

"Well I uhm," began Lloyd trying to select his words carefully, "I mean it wasn't actually assault. She simply swiped my lunch, made a lot of noise, caused some confusion among the other attendees and then I left."

"Oh" replied Officer Garland. "That's what happened is it?"

"Certainly" concluded Lloyd, glad that this was almost over. "Besides, I don't even want to press any charges, officer. I just want to forget about it and get some rest."

Officer Garland couldn't contain a chuckle, "Ha, ha!" He then relayed the joke to his fellow officers. "Hey guys, the man says he doesn't want to press charges."

Hotel security and the plain clothes officer joined in the laugher. This was not a comforting sound to Lloyd. Officer Garland quickly erased his smile and continued in a thoroughly professional tone, "I'll be sure to add that anecdote to my report Mr. Canard. Now, if you would be so kind as to turn around and place your hands behind your back."

He quietly complied without protest. He knew by now that things simply were not meant to go in his favor. Canard's quiet demeanor was understood to be an affirmation of guilt, so the officers discussed nothing more with him until they reached the station.

Lloyd sat calmly, shackled in handcuffs, and relayed his version of what occurred in the hotel's conference room. The officer asking questions rotated a couple times, but the questions remained the same. Good policemen that they were, they continued to pursue efforts to break the suspect so that his responses would match what they imagined had happened. Proper questioning wasn't part of the police officers' normal repertoire. Their usual mode of operation was to badger and wear the suspect down until he or she agreed with whatever they were instructed to confess to. Canard's answers became more labored from fatigue, but the details never wavered from his original statement.

\* \* \* \*

At home, Perla Canard was working the block with the zeal of a hyperactive greenhorn underneath the spotlights on Broadway for the very first time.  She made her way from house to house, banging on door after door, telling her ever-morphing story to anyone who would listen or those who were too polite to simply close their doors in her face.

Her horrifically exaggerated accusations and proclamations interrupted the usually peaceful neighborhood:

"My husband disappear!"

"He never call!"

"I know he have a mistress!"

"Maybe he have a whole nudder family!"

"Da police dey don help me nuthing!"

Several families had taken the extreme step of bolting the doors, closing the curtains, cutting off the television set and all lights to pretend that they were not home.  Perla was making such a spectacle of herself that three neighbors had called the police to report the nuisance.  But the police didn't arrive before the normally sedentary woman finally ran out of gas.  So dedicated was she to her imaginary acting career that she slumped, exhausted and dehydrated onto a lawn she was traversing.  Her sudden silence simultaneously answered the prayers and swears of many in the neighborhood.  The owner of the yard on which she eventually dropped was first motivated to drag her onto an adjacent property, but there were simply too many witnesses for that so he cursed his luck as he instead dialed for an ambulance.

The paramedics arrived with haste, and not having ever met an animated Perla Canard, they disappointed the gathering of onlookers by reanimating her without hesitation.  As she was loaded into the ambulance for transport, the residents resembled survivors of some great disaster.  They slowly emerged squinting in the sunlight from having been hiding inside darkened homes.  As the reverberation of the siren dwindled in the distance a spontaneous block party erupted.

Perla was transported to the hospital where she was encouraged to rest and underwent a thorough examination.  When the doctor on duty had received the results of several tests he went into consultation with Mrs. Canard.  Doctor McFarlane began with the usual spiel for this situation.  "It is of great importance to maintain proper hydration and avoiding strenuous outdoor activities during the hottest times of the day."

Then Doctor McFarlane became more personal and quite candidly told his patient, "Mrs. Canard I can tell you straight away that your diet is deplorable and it is effectively killing you."

"Aha!" yelled Perla as she hopped off the examining table and wagged her index finger accusingly in the face of the surprised doctor. "You don even know wat your talking about! I'm not even on a diet!"

The doctor was taken aback by this response, and after a brief moment to recompose from his surprise he replied, "Yes, well...that's what I'm speaking of. You do need to begin to pay attention to your diet so as to safeguard your health."

"Yeah, sure" she replied dismissively. She had already determined that this so-called medical professional was an absolute quack since he continued to insist that she was on a diet even after she'd clearly told him that she was not.

\* \* \* \*

As Barbara sat relaxing in her hotel room that evening, she was surprised to get another glance at the vicious anti-animal terrorist who had interrupted her peaceful PETA conference earlier in the day. There he was with his picture plastered across the evening news. A local station had obtained an amateur video clip of an unidentified man slapping a pigeon in a public park. She immediately recognized the offender, clear as rat droppings on a stick of butter, when she spotted the slothful silhouette of Lloyd Canard pounce to life with his insatiable appetite for attacking yet another innocent animal. After having witnessed firsthand the destruction this evil man was capable of, Barbara's sense of responsible citizenry prompted her to call the television station to identify this man so he could be prosecuted to the fullest extent of the law. Thorough as she was, she also checked the conference attendance records and found that Mr. Canard's registration and all fees had been paid by an employer. Bloated with both genuine concern that the streets of New York remain safe for piteous pigeon paupers, as well as the recent ingestion of an extra large Philly Cheese Steak Pizza from Dominos which she had discretely delivered to her room, Barbara thought it prudent to contact the man's employer to inform them of his disruptive criminal behavior and pending arrest.  She was completely unaware that the man she so despised was already in police custody.

It was Friday evening so Bitewoody senior management had already vacated for the weekend, but the security staff remained as always.  Coincidentally it was Security Supervisor Norma Fotheringham who was on duty and received the call from Barbara.  The message traveled from the exasperated woman in New York to the normally inattentive Fotheringham.  Mrs. Fotheringham perked up a bit as she heard the tale of Chief Canard's troubles.  She was aware that contacting Assistant Chief Brittle after hours for anything other than an extreme emergency was frowned upon, but she had a very strong feeling that he would want to hear this news as soon as possible.  Norma felt certain that being the first to deliver this spicy morsel of data would serve as an effective avenue to link herself to the rising king Brittle.

Russell Brittle was busy watching the beads of sweat roll across his biceps in the mirror when the call came in.  He was annoyed to be getting a call from the office on Friday night, but once Fotheringham shared the new information, his tune changed.  "We're going places Mrs. Fotheringham," he announced happily, "just grab hold of my tail and I'll pull you along!"

Norma didn't like the picture this weird invitation evoked and wasn't quite sure how to respond, so she simply closed the conversation with, "Thank you sir.  Have a nice weekend."

Brittle did a little victory dance in the mirror, and became distracted by the sight of his own flexing pectorals.  A few minutes later he snapped out of the stupor of self admiration and realized that he had to ensure upper management was aware of the disgraceful actions of their soon-to-be former chief of security.

It was a gleeful Russ Brittle who relayed the twisted tale to the dim-witted Bitewoody Vice President Steve Webster.  But somewhere along the line between Barbara the exasperated PETA representative; Fotheringham the absentminded security supervisor; Brittle the easily distracted narcissist; and the cerebrally deficient Webster, the information exchanged regarding recent events in New York had morphed into a totally unbelievable tale in which Canard, accompanied by a mime with a pigeon, had assaulted a cow with a hotdog.

Mr. Webster was absolutely flabbergasted at the report from the PETA conference. Having never realized Chief Canard's compulsive hatred of animals, he felt concerned that revelations about Canard's no longer secret animal hating acts might somehow reflect directly on him as an accomplice since it was he who had made the man attend the PETA conference. Without even stopping to think how ridiculous this scenario sounded, he continued in self-defense mode. He knew he had to report the allegations as soon as possible, so Webster found the business card in his briefcase and dialed the number for the police officer he'd met earlier that day.

Detective Fleenor was back in his office going over the details and multiple statements he'd collected earlier. He had run into a dead end with all the leads in the case. While Abel was far from understanding this Canard fellow, his instincts did tell him that there was something very suspicious here. Struck with a case of 'investigator's block' he had resorted to staring at the wall as if in a trance when the call from Steve Webster came in.

It was a beleaguered Fleenor who received this unexpected call with details of an unimaginably twisted tale. A desperate man can easily be duped and that's exactly the rationalization employed by this intellectually incurious investigator. He graciously accepted the gift as gospel without questioning legitimacy or dismissing any part of it as hearsay, since it fit quite well into the equally confusing profile he had already compiled on the miscreant Lloyd Canard. Abel now felt vindicated in his profiling of the suspect as a serial animal abuser. This confirmation of congruent clues coming together like properly placed puzzle pieces provided the encouragement he needed to ramp up the investigation and expand his reach by contacting New York area police. Fleenor had to be sure to get his name in on this investigation which now involved law enforcement officers in two states. Abel was well aware that the ensuing manhunt could easily span most of the east coast before eventually bringing this madman to justice. He was now even more determined to get to the bottom of this increasingly disgusting case.

\* \* \* \*

The television station's report of pigeon assault was received by the police while the culprit was still in custody. Though it wasn't anything the police would have normally pursued, they did broach the subject with the suspect. Canard's excuse that the bird had flown into his hand was laughably infantile. While it was not a chargeable offense, it did serve to further disgust the officers dealing with him.

When the evening meal came around for those in lockup, the officer serving Canard felt impelled to slap the tray out of his hands two seconds after passing it too him. Canard's eyes opened wide as he stared silently at the seething young cop.

"How did you like that?" demanded the officer.

"I didn't" answered Canard tersely.

"Now you know what it feels like!"

"How what feels like?"

"That pigeon that you slapped."

"Was that pigeon on the plate?" Lloyd inquired.

"No, it was chicken," the officer responded "but you know what I mean."

"Well I wasn't the one who killed it" Lloyd said in his own defense.

"You mean its dead?!" the shocked officer asked."

"I certainly hope so."

"You're a cruel, hateful man Canard."

"Well would you have served me a plate with live chicken?"

"I'm not talking about that bird on the floor; I'm talking about the one you struck in the park!"

"That stupid pigeon hit me" Lloyd explained uselessly.

"Oh man, you don't know how bad I want to come in that cell and slap you around."

Canard didn't respond to that. He figured being detained and hungry were bad enough without doing anything further to invite physical assault.

Sometime just before midnight, someone at the NYC police precinct had the brilliant idea to review the hotel surveillance tapes. This video evidence from the conference room clearly showed Lloyd sitting alone quietly until the large, aggressive woman approached, entered his personal space and began pestering him. Even without sound this visual evidence proved Lloyd's version of events. He could clearly be seen tripping over one of the folding chairs and falling into the unfortunate woman. More importantly, video from the hotel lobby recorded him departing with the hotdog in hand. This conclusively showed the investigating officers that Mr. Canard had in fact reached out with an open hand before tripping and falling into his taunting aggressor. Had he actually intended to strike the woman, his hand would have been closed tightly in a fist, and he never would have withdrawn with a handful of badly mauled hotdog.

# *** DAY SIX ***

# Saturday


It was past midnight when Lloyd was released from police custody for the second time in barely more than twenty-four hours. Though the police cleared him of any wrongdoing, they offered no apology as it was their position that Mr. Canard was completely at fault for having wasted *their* time. The less than esteemed police officers did see fit to admonish him to avoid the remainder of this weekend's PETA conference and either find an alternate hotel or simply return home to Fort Lauderdale as soon as possible. Lloyd was unhappy with the rude treatment from what he considered incompetent police, but had to agree with their conclusion. He had learned enough from his brief exposure to the PETA crowd to know that he would not benefit from a return to the conference or the same hotel. He was able to convince an officer to aid him in recovering his property from the room, but a call to the hotel informed them that nothing remained. Whatever hadn't been destroyed by the intruders had already been disposed of by hotel housekeeping. Lloyd shrugged his shoulders in reaction to this latest misfortune and gave a cursory thanks to the officer on his way out of the station. He departed the police station shaking his head. He had lost all previous trust and confidence in the legal system, particularly when it came to the supposed presumption of innocence and impartiality by police officers. If he was in fact, "fully cleared," as the police sergeant had so unconvincingly assured him, what purpose did their warning on departure to, "watch yourself next time or you might not be so lucky," serve unless they actually still believed he *had* to be guilty and had only escaped prosecution through some ingenious legal loophole known by the legal slang: 'incontrovertible innocence.' How could they claim to uphold the law, yet see themselves as sufficiently superior enough to skirt following legal procedures in seeking what they themselves loosely defined as justice?  He shuddered at the bravado of the police officers and their rather conspicuous disregard for the law.  He decided to cut his losses and try to put New York City behind him.  That was a pretty stupid expression in this case as he was fairly certain that almost everything that could possibly have gone wrong had already happened to him.  He had expected to find a land unlike any other in the Big Apple, but his actual experiences went mind bogglingly further than the worst he could have possibly ever imagined.

Canard was in dire need of a shower, change of clothes and a full night of uninterrupted rest, but even though B.E.O.T.C.H. had already paid for the hotel, he didn't seriously consider going back there.  Instead, he hailed a cab and asked the driver to take him to La Guardia Airport.  He tried not to dwell on the tornado of turmoil that had engulfed him during this brief visit to New York City, but instead set his sights on reaching the more familiar craziness of his own home.

All Canard had in his possession were the clothes on his back and the few personal articles he'd had in his pockets when detained by police.  He did receive a second look by airport security due to the rarity of someone traveling without any suitcases or property in their possession, but thankfully this time no one found the suspicion high enough to warrant wrestling him to the ground or having him stripped naked in front of a half dozen unqualified, undertrained security officers.

Having a couple hours to kill before his 4:00 AM departure, Lloyd made due with a sink bath in the airport men's room.  Of course he started by choosing a restroom with little traffic and absolutely no children present.  He did find some comfort from splashing water on his face and neck, but after donning the same dirty clothes once again that grimy, sticky feeling settled right back on him.

Once Lloyd had boarded the early morning flight and finally plopped down (or rather squeezed) into his middle seat, he promptly fell into a much-needed sleep.  His seat mates were disappointed at the profundity of his fatigue as Canard both snored loudly and slumped over on them repeatedly.  As annoyed as they were with what they considered to be his anti-social behavior, it only took a single look at his disheveled appearance and pigeon-poop-polka-dotted coat to determine that he was probably a raving nutcase. So the passengers seated nearest this annoying uproar sat quietly and thoughtfully refrained from disturbing this irritating man to avoid the possibility of causing him to throw a fit in flight.

* * * *

Detective Fleenor was also up early this Saturday morning. One of his favorite pastimes was early morning kayaking. This was his preferred method of escape from the stressful work environment. It was also a great way to avoid the crowded streets and malls where the majority of South Florida weekenders would inevitably gather. Those crowds were not for Abel, oh no. He'd opt for a long, hard row to work up a sweat then enjoy a comfortable paddle back inland before pausing to do a little fishing off the coast of Fort Lauderdale Beach. This athletic pursuit provided a comprehensive package of exercise, escape and the opportunity for silent solitude to ponder and pontificate on the bewildering case he was currently working. As Abel allowed his kayak to coast westward back towards the beach, the morning sun had just peeked over the horizon and warmly caressed his shoulders. He stowed his double ended oar, kicked back in the kayak with his feet propped up and leaned back with his eyes closed, utilizing the life vest as a pillow.

* * * *

Lloyd was wide awake now and fulfilling the fears forecast by his unfortunate seatmates. Alive with fright, he rocked back and forth in his cramped seat 24E. Just when he thought he had escaped the horrors of this disastrous trip he was forced to take, here he was trapped on a plane suffering severe mechanical problems. The flight had been expected to arrive on time until a problem with the landing gear appeared on final descent. The jet then circled out over the Atlantic Ocean for several minutes while the pilots worked to determine whether the problem was with the landing gear or simply the light which indicated that the gear was not properly locked into position. Fort Lauderdale Air Traffic Control and the pilots coordinated to clear the flight line and activate rescue personnel in preparation for an emergency landing.

As the huge Boeing 757 looped out over the Atlantic Ocean, the right wing dipped low as the pilot performed a wide turn. A very distraught passenger in 24E was able to get a clear look out the window. It was a beautiful day in Fort Lauderdale and there were already quite a few people staking claims on prime beach spots even at this early hour. Although he was certainly no fan of crowds, he wished very much that he could have been down there instead of up here in this malfunctioning plane. When a lone kayaker caught his eye he immediately wished he had the power to switch places with that lucky fellow enjoying the beauty of a summer day alone, drifting quietly away from the throngs of thongs on Fort Lauderdale Beach. Lloyd closed his eyes and tried to imagine he was that lone kayaker in peaceful, silent solitude.

* * * *

There was no breeze this morning, so the sea was smooth as glass and reflected the beautiful bright colors of the rising Sun. This beach was in the direct flight path of aircraft departing and arriving Fort Lauderdale Airport, so Abel was accustomed to the sounds of frequent air traffic. He ignored the distant drone of the powerful engines and did not realize that this particular jet was making its sixth pass 3500 feet above his head. Fleenor's fishing rod was loosely balanced across his stomach as he extracted and lit a cigar to aid in his relaxation. Abel took a deep breath of Dominican tobacco smoke and sea air; closed his eyes and exhaled strongly to clear his lungs as well as his mind.

* * * *

Lloyd dug his fingers deep into the armrest as he gyrated uncontrollably in his seat. The pilots had announced their intention to dump all excess fuel over the ocean before taking the disabled 757 in for an emergency landing. Canard couldn't help but envision an ugly outcome for this flight and was just short of wishing that he was still in New York City.

* * * *

Fleenor's quiet moment on the calm sea was interrupted by the terrific SPLASH!!! WHOOSH!!! SPLASH!!!

"YEEEEOOOOOWWWW!!!" noises that followed in quick, loud succession.

In a mere instant, Abel's world changed drastically. He had no clue as to what was happening, but he was almost simultaneously soaked with a powerful wave, engulfed in a fantastic, bright ball of flames and then drenched with an apparent second tidal wave. It all occurred in a fraction of a second as his body reacted badly to the rapid changes from a massive cold shower, to a fireball producing a surge of heat that would surely melt the clothing off his body, then almost instantly dashed with a cold wave of ocean water. He gasped desperately for clean air. He had the wind both knocked out of him and frightened out of him at the same time. Abel had never felt such an odd sensation, and he sat stunned and wondering if he had suffered some form of attack. His body tingled all over and a quick glance surprised him that the skin covering his arms was completely hairless and bright pink, looking somewhat equivalent to a fairly intense sunburn. His hair and mustache were badly singed and his eyebrows were almost nonexistent. His head was filled with questions, but not a single sensible answer. Something was incredibly wrong. He began to notice a roaring noise increasing in volume. Abel turned and saw a motorboat racing towards him. His automatic reaction was to wave his arms and shout, "Slow down, slow down! Kayaker here, keep the wake down!" But the boat pressed on at an alarmingly high speed directly towards him.

'So this is how it's going to end' he thought almost nonchalantly. He offered no resistance and easily accepted what he expected would be a quick and immediate departure from this cruel world. The speeding boat cut its engine several yards away and in the silence he noticed a loud ringing in his ears. The boat drifted forward until making contact with his kayak.

Fleenor yelled defensively, "What are you doing? Can't you see me sitting right here?!"

The boater's mouth hung open wide as he leaned over the bow and asked, "Are you okay? Are you hurt?"

Fleenor hadn't yet worked out what had happened, and wasn't really thinking properly. He supposed that he might have just experienced a rare case of spontaneous human combustion, but thought it more likely that an underwater gas line had burst or maybe a large manatee had farted beneath his boat and the vapors had ignited from his cigar ash. Evidently the detective's keen perception was at the normal level and his desire to unravel the mystery was comforted by the hope that this witness might be able to aid in his determination of what exactly had just occurred. The stranger maneuvered his craft alongside the kayak and extended his hand to assist Fleenor. As he allowed the man to help him from the kayak into his motorboat, he sensed a very strong odor of fuel. A snap of alarm caused Fleenor to ask the captain, "Do you have a fuel leak?"

"No" the man answered confidently. "What makes you ask that?"

"Can't you smell that?" Fleenor asked incredulously. "I can definitely smell a very strong odor of fuel."

"Oh yeah, I do smell *that,* "the man answered, "but it's you man. You just got doused by a load of jet fuel."

"What does that mean?" Fleenor asked as he tried to understand what nautical interpretation the man's last phrase might have.

"You got in the way of the fuel dumped by that jet plane and when it hit you it burst into flames" the man said excitedly. From his statement, it seemed that he blamed Fleenor for being the victim.

"What...but...how?" the crispy kayaker stammered in total confusion. He managed to ask, "Is something burning?" before succumbing to the fumes, burns and circumstances, and finally lost consciousness.

* * * *

The plane landed in Fort Lauderdale among great fanfare, but without serious trouble. There were no injuries greater than the split eardrums suffered by several passengers from the inhumanly high pitched screams of the high school cheerleading squad that filled the several rows immediately behind them. Eager to get this horrible trip behind him, Lloyd unthinkingly stood up too quickly and banged his head on the overhead baggage compartment. As his unconscious body folded limply onto the lap of his seatmate, the laughter waned only slightly. The man on whose lap he now lay stood up abruptly and allowed Lloyd's unconscious body to slump onto the floor. The stranger shook his head at the stupidity of the man now lying still on the floor between seats; but he wore a small smile of appreciation that at least the man wasn't snoring so obnoxiously this time.  The selfish, uncaring individuals aboard the plane from New York City all pretended not to notice the man's body on the floor as they exited the plane.  No questions were asked and no assistance was offered.  Finally a flight attendant spotted Lloyd on the floor and tried to wake him with a rough shake.  She suspected he was drunk, but when he didn't respond to the shake or even a kick to the head, the flight attendant ceased her creative version of first aid and called for paramedics.  The aggravated flight attendant plopped down hard in an adjacent seat, and cursed the unconscious man for creating more paperwork and preventing her departure for home.

* * * *

Detective Fleenor was rudely awakened by a hideous sound.  He was surprised to find himself encased in bandages and his eyes covered with gauze.  It took several seconds for him to recognize he was in a hospital room.  He slowly recalled the vague circumstances that led to his arrival here.  Then his eardrums were again pummeled by that horrid sound.  It was a voice that grated harshly on his nerves yet seemed oddly familiar.  Abel shook noticeably when he finally realized it was the voice of Perla Canard that had so horribly harkened him from a serious slumber.  Annoying as the sound was, the detective was interested to hear that she was loudly asking questions about the location and condition of her husband.  He didn't really consider why Canard might be in the hospital, but was more intrigued by the opportunity to finally see and confront this sick, demented excuse for a man.  Abel could hear that woman peppering the physician with questions so clearly because they were standing just outside the door.  Although he was alone at the moment, Fleenor did not have a private hospital room.  Whether you blame it on pure chance, substandard health insurance or the humorous manipulations of some deviant deity, it happened that both Fleenor and Canard were assigned to the same small convalescent room in the hospital.  A nurse came in and spoke briefly with Abel to discuss his injuries and explain their planned treatment.  To help with the pain, the nurse added some additional pain medication to his intravenous drip.

As Lloyd was being wheeled back towards the room from x-ray, he began to come to.  He was disoriented, and though he could feel the sensation of movement, he was unable to move any part of his own body.  He didn't realize that his head, neck, spine and every limb had been immobilized to ensure he didn't further injure himself.  He barely parted his eyelids and could see that he was lying on his back and apparently being rolled down a long white hallway with fluorescent lighting.  Between the knot on his head and the drugs administered in the hospital, he flitted in and out of consciousness.  He was never really able to remain awake long enough to work out everything that was going on though he easily deduced that he was in a hospital.  This seemed a good sign as he figured that if he had come through the plane crash with enough to salvage and transport to a hospital then at least he had a chance of survival.

Fleenor was fast asleep before Canard's unconscious body was brought back into the room.  There were only a couple feet separating the two men, but they were each still completely unaware of the other's presence.

The orderlies had to manipulate the stretcher, to which Lloyd was fastened, back onto the bed.  It was a difficult task to balance this awkward weight and move the fragile cargo so carefully, but the procedure was accomplished by a small, powerful pulley system installed in the ceiling.  The stretcher was securely attached, lifted upwards, and then twisted around to achieve the best position to replace the patient squarely on the bed.  Because of the cramped space in the small room, this effort resulted in the stretcher having to be temporarily tilted slightly to one side.  It just so happened that at this same moment Lloyd's eyelids fluttered and he awoke.  He was only conscious for a few seconds, but it was perfectly timed so that when he opened his eyes, the view he had was of the bandage covered body of Abel Fleenor lying on the bed below him.  Even in this brief semiconscious state Lloyd realized what he was witnessing: he had just died and his spirit was rising out of his badly disfigured body.  He closed his eyes and tried to come to the realization that he was dead and ascending to heaven.  Suddenly he sensed something different.  He reopened his eyes and saw that he was no longer rising, but was now actually descending. As the well-lubricated pulley silently lowered him past the motionless, bandaged body on the bed, he clenched his eyes shut in regret for not having lived a better life. The severe panic and dread combined with the ominous revelation of such a frightful sight caused Lloyd to black out once more.

An unknown amount of time later, Lloyd slowly regained consciousness and realized that he was on a thin cot in a small room. He appeared to be alone and the only sound he could detect was a rhythmic electronic chirping every twenty seconds or so. Though his body was still laid out on the slab, it made no sense that he had returned rather than moving on. He tried to move, but couldn't. He didn't understand what that meant or why the annoying beeping of the machine persisted when his earthly body had already expired. So why hadn't his soul yet departed? That's when his last vision before passing out flashed through his head. He was alarmed at the fact that he had initially begun ascending, but then had been abruptly rerouted in the opposite direction. Where was he now? Did purgatory wait outside the door to this small room? Was he in some sort of limbo awaiting final decision? If his case was so borderline, was there anything he might do to improve his chance towards a heavenly eternity? Unsure what to do, or if doing anything was even an option at this point, he closed his eyes and silently prayed that he might be spared an infinite punishment. He offered to be a better person if he could just have one more chance to make a positive difference in the crazy world he had just departed.

Medical exams and x-rays found nothing seriously wrong with Lloyd, but since he kept losing consciousness, the doctors decided to keep him overnight for precautionary observation. The remainder of his day was spent in a concussion-induced haze, where he was restlessly pestered by the same worrying dream of eternal damnation.

## *** DAY SEVEN ***

## Sunday

Canard eased out of his slumber and became aware of the bright red color showing through his eyelids.  He very cautiously opened his eyes and saw what appeared to be a large fluorescent light over his head.  He blinked his eyes several times in an effort to focus his vision.

"You're back!" Perla exclaimed accusatorily.

He jumped at the sound of a voice in the room then winced even more at the realization that it was his wife's angry tone.  Confused and disoriented he replied only, "Yes dear."

Quicker at detecting clues than Fleenor, Perla Canard immediately recognized Lloyd's deference as an admission of guilt.  With a sly smile of conquest on her lips, Perla shot back with, "So, where deed you go?" in a tone he sensed as noticeably more incriminating than enthusiastic about his return.

"I'm not sure" he answered honestly.

Since Lloyd assumed that he had already died, he guessed that this scenario was a challenge of the promise he'd made in recent prayer.  Having heard of Satan's fabled treachery, he was not surprised that the devious demon had chosen to reveal himself in the form of Perla in an attempt to win everlasting control of his soul.  Intending to play it safe, he held his tongue and tried to measure his responses very delicately.  He certainly didn't want to fail this final test and be forever cast into the depths of infernal purgatory.

"Not sure, huh?" she registered her disbelief in those three simple words.

"No. Not really" he admitted thoughtfully.  "But I think it would best be described as limbo."

"Where da hell ez dat?!" she asked.  "It sound made up to me.  Maybe you wan to sey you were wid some bimbo!"

"What?" was all he could muster to respond in his physically subdued and philosophically overactive condition. He wasn't sure whether he was more bothered by having her stand over his hospital bed and make such ridiculous accusations or the mere fact that she'd have a word like 'bimbo' in her limited English vocabulary. He'd just managed to somehow survive a plane crash and here she was looming over his apparently fresh deathbed and continuing right where she'd left off with her crazy, nonsensical accusations of infidelity. Boy, this was really tricky. He couldn't be certain yet whether this was his real wife or some evil apparition conjured by Satan to taunt him into failing the final opportunity of his pitiful life. He remained quiet for a moment and tried hard to figure out what he should do next. Perla didn't appreciate his silence as she'd been itching for confrontation. Her husband's muteness only pissed her off even more, so she launched into a tirade of hateful allegations: "You disappear from your family, run off with some woman named Felynn! Yes, dats right I know about her! You never even call home once. Your wife get sick from worry an your own sweet little daughter miss her papi so much dat she can't even focus on her homework; she only sit and stare at television for hours and hours!"

Lloyd's only response was a heavy sigh and a huge grin. While he didn't understand half of what his wife was talking about, he did now have clear confirmation that he'd made it back home: alive even if not quite well. Lucifer would have been much better informed about his actual life and recent travails and never would have included such outlandishly unbelievable accusations and assertions. Only the real Perla Canard could have fashioned such an unreasonably elaborate tale portraying herself as a model wife and Andi as a perfectly sweet little daddy's girl who desperately longed to choose homework over television. She was temporarily at a loss for words from her husband's impertinence. Lloyd took advantage of this brief gap and told her, "I think I need to rest," in a tired, weak sounding voice. Before she could recoup and protest, an unknown male voice intruded on their conversation: "Actually, I think it would be best if you could give me a few minutes alone with your husband Mrs. Canard." Lloyd was surprised to hear another voice in the small room, but was thankful for the stranger's intervention. In a rare moment of deference, Perla quietly complied with the man's request and left the room without pause or protest. This immediately alerted Lloyd that the man in the room must be a doctor here to deliver considerably grave news about the injuries he'd sustained in the plane crash. This assumption was soon challenged when he caught a strained glimpse of the stranger who appeared to be wearing a hospital gown. The unknown man had no visible facial hair, gauze patches over both his eyes and his skin appeared to be very bright red and covered in some type of thick, clear gel.

Canard and Fleenor: Two men, whose lives had so recently become intimately intertwined, now found themselves face-to-face for the first time. Well, not quite face-to-face considering Lloyd was only able to use his peripheral vision since the brace prevented him from turning to look towards Fleenor directly, and Abel's view of his quarry was largely hampered by peering through gauze covered eyes.

Lloyd supposed that the man was a burn victim and probably another survivor from the plane crash, but he was still very confused by the way Perla had acquiesced to his request for a private conversation. Abel would appear to have been positioned with the upper hand in this encounter, except that both his vision and his perspective were hampered. The detective was working with an extremely distorted profile of the type person he thought Canard to be. Fleenor had formulated a fabulously fictitious profile of the man lying before him based on totally misreading all the misinformation he had improperly identified as being relevant. Lloyd stared cluelessly at the bandaged face by his bed, and though he had no idea of what the stranger wanted to talk about, the odd twist of the man's mouth seemed to indicate that it would not be a friendly conversation.

Abel closed the door after Perla's departure and introduced himself: "I am Detective Fleenor of the Fort Lauderdale Police Department and I want to talk with you regarding a number of disturbing reports on your recent activities."

Before Canard could respond Fleenor held up the flat palm of his hand and stated: "To start off, let me explain that this is a one-sided conversation." Having ostentatiously set the stage for a completely useless interview, the detective proceeded to expound on all the things he imagined this man was guilty of. Canard's current condition rendered him incapable of responding with the body language he'd like to present in this situation. Unable to stand with a rebellious posture and arms folded across his chest, Lloyd did his best to signify doubt and defiance with raised eyebrows and pursed lips. As instructed, he simply stared at the blabbering investigator who he felt must certainly be emotionally unstable. Detective Fleenor wasted this opportunity as he was simply too enthralled with his own grand ideas to actually pose any questions or make a single inquiry of his primary suspect.

Although Perla was annoying, at least Lloyd was accustomed to her usual range of accusations. This masked man was going on about things so eccentric that he thought for sure that rather than being a police detective he must have wandered away from the hospital's psychiatric ward. Fleenor's odd line of reasoning seemed to touch on several unrelated events that did have some connection to Canard's life such as the dead cat incident, the fish bowl imprisonment, casino cashier complaint, PETA conference problems, hotdog assault, pigeon slapping, mix up in the pedophile sting and the long list of accusations by Perla. But the manner in which the detective strung these random incidents together, as if they were all pieces of some master plot designed to ultimately disable an airplane on which Lloyd himself was traveling was absolutely absurd.

Canard dared not speak out of turn as his words were not at all relevant to this silly little man's intrepid grasp of the 'facts' as he had built them from the tiny pieces of unconnected information he imagined were actual clues. Lloyd was horrified at the accusations, but realized that the investigator's claims were so far-fetched that they would not likely result in any type of conviction. In fact, if any judge ever got wind of all this, it would most likely be Fleenor that ended up being dragged away in custody.

Seemingly uninvolved in his own interrogation, Lloyd allowed his mind to drift away from this intentionally one-sided conversation to replay the two other recent interactions he'd had with law enforcement. Obviously he had come away from these encounters with more suspicion than trust. He no longer had confidence in either the police to do what was right or the legal system to function as a protective shield for the common citizen. Had Canard himself not been the focus of this man's misguided ire, he might have had a laugh at the way the detective's voice rose in despair and his eyes widened in unison with each new charge. It was as if the very words spewing from his own mouth were just as much a surprise to the speaker as they were to the unsuspecting victim.  Listening to Fleenor's rant made Canard feel almost as if he was hearing multiple channels broadcasting simultaneously on the radio as the questions, pieces of information and blatant allegations appeared to be completely random and unconnected. But as his headache seemed to find a new capability to excavate even more deeply into his brain, he unfortunately did realize the connection.  As random and ridiculous as it sounded, he knew that these seemingly unrelated details were actually connected by a common thread.  That commonality was Lloyd Canard himself. Who else but he could live such a disastrous life?  While Canard easily understood that this was just one week in his mostly unlucky lifetime, it wasn't so simple to explain that fact to an outsider. Even his own wife had never accepted the truth about how fate and nature constantly conspired to taunt and annoy him.  How in the world could Lloyd ever explain to this blabbering police detective that this past week's events were nothing out of the ordinary for him?  Detective Fleenor was only a pedestrian; a simple passerby who circumstance led to glance briefly into the world of turmoil where Lloyd Canard dwelt.  Abel's vista was but a brief view through the window into the obtuse realm of constant confusion and trouble where he spent his entire life.

Fleenor's mouth was running and Canard's head was spinning as he tried to keep up with this man's irrational train of thought.  The detective finished his tirade by adding the exciting coup de grace in which he exposed: "And then to cover your tracks you attempted to take out the lead investigator by dousing him in highly flammable jet fuel!"

Lloyd no longer stared at his inquisitor with a look of defiance.  His eyes were now wide open and glazed over, while the muscles of his lips had given in and served only to frame his mouth which hung in wide open, wordless surprise.

Fleenor was feeling much better now; hardly noticing his burns at all as he irrationally complimented Canard.  "It was indeed a spectacular plan that you very nearly pulled off with flawless accuracy!"

'Flawless' and 'Accuracy' were two words that Lloyd Canard rarely ever heard, and they made absolutely no sense at all when strung together as a summary of the events which had transpired during this past week of endless disaster, bedlam and misunderstanding.

So sure of himself was Detective Fleenor that he believed any information, which might have been gleaned from a proper interview with his main suspect, would be useless in affecting the result of his investigation. Abel had his expected outcome already etched in the stone which sat in the vacant space that was meant to contain his brain.

Lloyd couldn't figure this guy out. Was he actually a trained detective? How could an experienced investigator fail to query the most ludicrous data which he'd found and solely determined to be true, without question, confirmation, collaboration or investigation? Lloyd wondered whether this strange man who seemed to know way too much about him might actually present a danger.

Canard was neither offered the opportunity to explain things to this man nor was he capable of getting out of bed and leaving. Lloyd also knew that the detective's departure would only allow Perla to come back in and resume her own interrogation. If there was one thing life had prepared him for it was the ability to ignore his less than amiable surroundings. Out of both patience and options, Canard decided to play opossum and pretended to fall back asleep.

＊ ＊ ＊ ＊

After release from the hospital Sunday afternoon, Lloyd had Perla drive him to the airport to retrieve his car. During this time he was cornered and forced to listen to his wife's interminable harangue concerning all of the stuff he was suspected of having done recently. But on this occasion he actually did pay attention because the detailed misperceptions that occurred during his absence were mind boggling. Perla was bad enough on her own, but teamed up with Fleenor and Liz they had devised evermore outlandish tales of the escapades Lloyd must have been up to. He was also very surprised to find out that he had not been in a plane crash at all. As disturbing as all the details were, it did provide him with useful background information on where and how the detective's ludicrous accusations had emerged.

Perla even blamed Lloyd for causing it all. "Eef you had a more positive attitude you wouldn't cause all dis bad stuff to happen."

"I don't have a bad attitude, I..." Lloyd began before being interrupted by a loud snort of doubt from his wife. He continued, "...I only have a realistic expectation that bad things will happen based on the accumulated experiences of my entire life."

"Dats whut I'm talkin' about!" exclaimed Perla.

Lloyd paused before summarizing, "I guess you mean that if I only think of good things then my life will magically become better."

"Eets not magic, eets just true."

"Well it sounds to me like trying to live in some kind of fantasy world." He then suggested jokingly, "Maybe I should see a hypnotist."

"For ju, maybe eet wurk" Perla agreed heartily, not having realized that this far out suggestion was made in jest.

When they arrived at Fort Lauderdale Airport the car was not where Lloyd had parked it. He spent forty minutes running around and jumping through all sorts of bureaucratic hoops to find the appropriate authority that eventually relayed the information that his automobile had been towed. Once in possession of the data, he called the towing company to ask for directions. He was told that their business was only half-open on Sundays.

"Do you mean you are only open a half-day on Sunday?"

"No, we half open all day" the man attempted to explain in poor English.

Whatever meaning that statement had was lost to Lloyd, so he asked bluntly, "May I pick up a car that was towed from Fort Lauderdale Airport today?"

"No car towed today" the man on the phone responded.

"No, I'm sorry, I was unclear," he apologized, "the vehicle was towed last week, but I'd like to pick it up today."

"No, I already tell you it no open today."

Exasperated with this man's insufficient ability to communicate, Lloyd demanded impatiently, "Then why are you there answering the telephone if you're closed?"

"Only tow on Sunday," the man explained, "no release car Sunday...half open."

"Okay" he huffed, finally understanding the man's encrypted message. "What time do you open in the morning?"

"Seven o'clock."

Lloyd hung up abruptly hoping that he'd not have to deal with the same moron tomorrow morning.

# *** DAY EIGHT ***

## Monday

     Lloyd began his Monday with the dreaded task of taking a cab to the towing service storage lot to retrieve his car.  Once he identified himself he was attended to rather promptly, as the managers of the lot were exceedingly glad to be getting rid of the thing.

     "Having that smelly thing on the lot is just bad for business" one of the men told him.  Yes, the car did stink to high heaven Canard agreed, but to claim that it cast a dark cloud on the usual sunny atmosphere of a locale which was primarily a junkyard was quite a bit of a stretch.

     Canard pulled into the first shopping center he passed and disposed of the dead cat as well as the uniform shirt he'd taken back from Gonzalo.  He then drove to the office with all the windows down and breathed as little as he could.  He planned to take advantage of the auto detailing services provided through Bitewoody Hotel valet parking.  B.E.O.T.C.H. employees received a twenty percent discount, and though he'd never used it before, he was sure the service would be well worth the expense today.  As he turned into the entrance of the Bitewoody Center, he felt his stomach do a flip; or maybe what he experienced would be better described as a flop.  He had mixed feelings about returning to work after all that had happened.  Honestly he had mixed feelings about returning to work every day, but this was a little different as he had been through so much recently that he was concerned his activities and misfortunes might overwhelm the rumor mill and possibly result in lockjaw for some of the more officious chin-waggers.  The day to day gossip was bad enough, but after the cat, the pigeon, the fat PETA lady, the hotdog attack, the arrest for suspected pedophilia, the injury on the plane, the hospitalization and Fleenor's exaggerated accusations, he simply did not know what to expect.  Lloyd was pretty certain that all things considered, this could very well turn out to be one of his worse days at work ever.

BUMP, THUMP, SMASH!!!

Lloyd hit the brakes in response to the noise and jolting movement of the car.  He knew right away that he had hit something.  Now his stomach really did a somersault as his mind raced with the tragic events that would follow if he had hit another cat.  He almost hoped to find a human body under his car instead.  He jumped out of the car quickly, not out of concern for whatever might be injured, but hoping that he might fix or escape from the problem before anyone could see what happened.  Peering under the vehicle he saw a pile of garbage.  Then a few items came into better focus.  "Aaarrrggghhh!" he squalled in frustration.  This was worse than hitting either a person or a cat.  He realized he had just destroyed the ridiculous memorial someone had erected in remembrance of the deceased feline!  He felt the familiar stabbing pain creeping into his temples as he attempted to quickly dislodge the wooden cross, wreath, flowers, stuffed animals and assorted debris from underneath his smelly automobile.

Canard's time away from B.E.O.T.C.H. was meant to be a break to allow a cooling down period for fanatic employees to forget their emotional reactions to the ridiculous cat incident.  Instead of slipping back in quietly and unnoticed, Lloyd began attracting negative attention before he could even reach the front door.  There was no way he could cover up the strewn pieces of the kitty memorial his car had just demolished.  He wondered what kind of idiot would set this crap up in the most inconvenient spot near the entrance of the parking lot.  Then he noticed that some comedian had drawn a chalk outline on the unfortunate cat's final resting place.  On closer inspection Lloyd discovered that it wasn't actually chalk, but paint; which would serve to remind everyone of this whole catastrophe for a whole lot longer.  He tried to think who to blame, but the more he thought of it the longer the list of probable guilty parties grew.  Why wouldn't his officers put half the effort into their jobs as they did into stupid antics like this that were in no way related to their security duties?  He lowered his head and sighed with the acknowledgement that the cat incident would not blow over quickly.

He finally made it past the former memorial and dropped his car off with the valet. He witnessed the grimace of the young man who flinched from the stench of the odorous vehicle, but pretended not to notice. Chief Canard's worry over the certain outcry that would result from his destroying the flat kitty memorial was quickly forgotten when he saw what looked to be the former Officer Gonzalo inside Post One chatting with the officer on duty. He quickly switched channels from concern to anger. He walked up and banged on the glass and shouted, "Hey, don't you know you aren't supposed to have visitors on post? Particularly of the *civilian* kind!" He added that last part as an intentional insult to Adrian Gonzalo who he completely blamed for this whole crazy cat business and the ensuing horrible week of extraordinary misadventures.

The uniformed officer on duty looked at him with a dumbfounded glare of confusion. Then Gonzalo turned around sporting a huge friendly smile as he greeted, "Good morning sir, nice to have you back with us."

Lloyd's brain flickered momentarily much like the screen used to flicker as the old movie reels reached the end of tape. He wondered how long he'd actually been gone or if he'd somehow slipped into an alternate dimension upon return. Gonzalo exited Post One with the same stupid grin across his face and walked towards him with his right hand outstretched in greeting. Lloyd reflexively extended his own hand, and as he watched Gonzalo take his hand and shake it aggressively, he felt like he was having an out of body experience. He didn't seem in control of his hand, but felt more like he was instead watching the event from afar. Maybe this sensation was an effect of his head injury, or possibly just the shock of returning to work again. Whatever the cause, it was not aided by seeing the name tag sported by his enthralled greeter, which prominently read: "Adrian Gonzalo – B.E.O.T.C.H. Security Supervisor."

Lloyd suddenly felt very lightheaded. His torso buckled and knees quivered weakly as if he might pass out. He shuffled his feet in an attempt to maintain his balance as the room began to spin around him. Gonzalo kept hold of his right hand and quickly placed his left hand on the chief's elbow to steady him. Another officer appeared out of the woodwork and placed a hand at

Canard's lower back to prevent his toppling over. The two men guided him helpfully to a nearby chair.

"We heard about your accident Chief," Gonzalo said before soothingly suggesting, "Do you think you may be returning to work too soon?"

Lloyd had no doubt that his return was too soon, but he simply shook his head side to side and took a deep breath before answering, "No, I'm alright. Just a little woozy I think."

"Why don't you just sit for a minute" Gonzalo suggested. "By the way, let me introduce you to my cousin who just started with us today."

Lloyd half-heartedly turned and gave a weak greeting to the new officer. Something slowly clicked in his befuddled brain and he did a double take, looking back at the oddly familiar face of the new officer.

"Chief, this is Oscar Reyes" introduced Gonzalo proudly. "Officer Reyes, this is our Chief of Security, Mr. Lloyd Canard."

Canard stared back at him wordlessly.

"Oscar comes to us directly from TSA, so his training with Homeland Security should be a great asset to B.E.O.T.C.H.'s security team."

Of course. Now Lloyd knew why the face seemed familiar: this was the officer who'd tackled him last Thursday at Fort Lauderdale Airport. He wasn't surprised at all that the goofball was related to Adrian Gonzalo or that fate had chosen to deliver this incompetent pair to meet him on his return to the office.

The newbie Security Officer Reyes evidently recognized his new boss as well. That was clear from the ridiculous ear-to-ear grin frozen on his face that was wholly at odds with the fright-enlarged pupils staring from below his sweat laden, deeply wrinkled forehead.

Lloyd lowered his head towards his knees, shook his head from side to side in frustration and allowed a low, deep growl to emit from his throat. He couldn't splice enough neurons nor accumulate sufficient energy to formulate a verbal response at this point. He rose and walked away without making eye contact with any of the curious onlookers in the lobby.

So this was how he learned that Brittle had not only rescinded Gonzalo's firing, but had actually promoted him to supervisor. Brittle later explained it as a proactive move he thought would quell an anticipated legal action for being fired in response to openly supporting animal rights. Lloyd further learned that Webster and upper management supported the move and frowned upon Canard for even questioning what they had oddly coined a, "positively progressive change." He didn't understand what they meant by that at all, but he wasn't concerned enough to ask; or even resist. Lloyd knew when he'd been beaten. Life had certainly engrained that lesson into him several times before.

He thought it might help to splash a little cold water on his face before attempting to recover and resume work. As he was walking down the hallway towards the restroom, he passed the night shift Supervisor Norma Fotheringham on her way out of the women's bathroom. When they locked eyes her face immediately burst into a huge grin. This was surprise enough until she added with a devilish smile, "Enjoy your coffee sir."

He responded with a reflexive, "Thank you," but was more focused on her suspicious grin. The laughter he heard once she'd rounded the corner only added to his discomfort. As he was about to open the door to the men's room, the ladies room door opened again and out walked Miss Jordan holding his coffee pot in her hand. He felt this was more than just coincidence so he asked, "What do you have there Miss Jordan?"

"I'm on the way to make your coffee sir."

He couldn't leave it alone. "Have you any idea why Ms. Fotheringham just came out of the ladies room laughing?"

"Oh she was just like, making fun of me because she saw me filling your carafe with water."

"What could she possibly find so funny about that?" he inquired suspiciously.

"I'm not really sure Mr. Canard," she responded in her annoyingly high-pitched voice, "I guess she just thought I like, looked silly scooping it out like that."

"Scooping it out?" he asked with obvious alarm. "What do you mean scooping *out* the water?"

"Well, the only way to fill your coffee pot it is to like, scoop the water from the toilet bowl" she explained innocently.

Lloyd's eyes bulged in surprise as he struggled with this revelation. "Why in the world would you do that?!"

"Well, the sinks are too like, shallow to fit the carafe so I have to dip the water to fill it."

"And you see nothing wrong with that?!" The despair was ripe in his voice as he struggled to comprehend this distasteful discovery.

Seeing the look of horror on the Chief's face, Liz smiled confidently and shook her head as if dismissing his concern. Then with her cute dimpled cheeks, nerdy glasses and squeaky voice she consoled him by saying, "Don't worry Mr. Canard, I always flush twice before scooping out the water for your coffee; three times if there are still like, particles floating around."

"Always?" was all he could manage to respond. He felt sick. Very sick. And thoroughly betrayed.

"Of course," she assured him "I promise." "Besides, once the water boils it destroys any germs."

He paused. "But the water doesn't boil in a coffee pot, it only warms up."

"Really?" she posed with tilted head. "I didn't know that. Well thank goodness it goes through that filter. I guess that's what like, makes it safe to drink."

"It's not that kind of filter."

"Well, I don't know the like, mechanics of it, but something seems to work" she concluded mindlessly.

"How long..." he struggled through his nausea to finish the question, "how long have you been using that water for my coffee?"

"The whole time" she answered, still unaware of any problem, "and don't worry, I'll have this ready for you in like, about ten minutes."

Lloyd watched in shock as Miss Jordan walked down the hall with his bucket of toilet water. The sexy little intern no longer carried the same appeal for him. Her smile had lost its charming, mesmerizing gleam. He now saw only a stupid child before him; the blinders had been removed and he could see the true depth of her ignorance. She had revealed herself to be just another part of the machinery which ran constantly, and at a frantic pace to produce an overwhelming amount of stupidity in this world. Elizabeth Jordan had just been transferred to Canard's useless idiot list.

Miss Jordan left the fresh-brewed toilet coffee in the pot by the door to Canard's office, and although it smelled good, he had no desire to drink it. Maybe he'd just give up on coffee altogether...but probably not.  More likely he'd resort to bringing coffee from home or buying a cup along the way into work.  Having had so much recent illumination on the nature of life, the absurdity of people and from being the constant victim of circumstances, he was pretty depressed with this new clearer, yet bleaker outlook on life in general and with his miserable life in particular.

Canard sat in his office frozen in thought.  His mind replayed the past week's events and he attempted to find some logical reason behind it all.  Liz noticed her boss's demoralized state and realized he must be suffering some injury or lingering trauma from his accident on the plane and time in hospital.  She felt sorry for Mr. Canard and took the extra step of filling his coffee mug and setting it on the desk before him.  She said nothing and he made no indication that he even noticed her in the room.  The intern quietly left him to his thoughts.  His mentations ran through his recent experiences and tried to make sense of it.  Any of it.

"Are they all mad?" Lloyd whispered out loud to himself, "or is it really just me who has the problem?"

The truth was that he really didn't feel very well.  The revelation about his morning coffee certainly had something to do with it, but that wasn't all.  Lloyd wasn't just physically ill, he also felt completely beaten down by life.  Why was it that everyone and everything seemed to be against him?  Was his role in the universe to be nothing more than the repository of bad luck?  He was sincerely dumbfounded by his position in life.  He sat quietly for a moment pondering the possibilities.  His eyes settled on the vase for a moment, and while the plant looked quite healthy he was unable to see the little red fish.  He watched for a moment to see if it would reappear from behind the roots, and then accepted the fact that it was no longer there.  Canard's first thought was whether it was possible that the plant had overpowered and consumed the diminutive fish, but he decided it was more likely that someone had set the damn thing free in his absence.  He doubted that the domesticated creature would be able to survive in the wild.  Then he considered that the alternative of being confined to that jar in this small room was no way to spend one's life either.  Feeling some solidarity with the animal now, Lloyd hoped the ugly little fish could enjoy his new freedom, find some adventure or maybe even encounter a friendly, bug-eyed female fish before inevitably becoming a larger fish's lunch. He blinked his eyes, came out of the trance and looked at the clock: it was 8:11 AM. Canard dropped his head in anguish, let out a lungful of air in a huge sigh of surrender and was in such a state of confusion with meandering thoughts and mental distractions that simply out of habit he lifted the mug to his lips and took a large gulp of the dark, special coffee before realizing his mistake.

On his way to the 8:15 AM morning meeting, Lloyd noticed a variety of reactions to his presence from several of the people he passed in the hallways. Some gave him hateful stares and some just looked the other way, but others clearly looked at him with sympathy. He guessed that each individual had their own reaction to whichever story they had heard from this very busy past week. Lloyd had hoped that he could slip back into his routine quietly and unnoticed, but that was too much to wish for. He had already heard enough of the rumors himself to know that while his absence had not gone unnoticed, it was actually celebrated by some.

The morning meeting kicked off with a handshake and, "Welcome back Chief," from Mr. Bitewoody. This cordiality was followed by the CEO's impersonation of a mime trapped in a box. Everyone laughed except Canard, Webster and Bigglio. Lloyd took the empty chair between the two of them. As the room was distracted by a couple other jokers pretending to be mimes, Webster leant over and told Lloyd harshly, "You really got me in a bind this time!"

"What are you talking about?"

"I stuck my neck out to get you that sweet assignment to New York, and then you repaid me by creating all kinds of mayhem up there!"

"You stuck your neck out?" Lloyd questioned in startled disbelief. "It was *you* who came up with the idea of sending me to that loony place as a form of punishment, and *you* who forced me to go against my will. If anybody's neck was sticking out, then it was certainly mime...I mean *mine*!"

Mr. Webster's eyes immediately widened in surprise and then slowly narrowed with anger. He didn't respond to the insubordinate comment, but Canard felt certain that he'd hear about it later. Lloyd's eyes connected with Giovanni, and the message clearly conveyed from his friend was yet another look of pity. At least he knew that this one was sincere. As the meeting about nothing began, he pulled himself into his protective shell and his mind left the room where his body remained for the useless assembly.

After the meeting Canard walked almost zombie-like down the hallway. He was interrupted by the appearance of Security Supervisor Nick Swath.

"Hey Chief, it's great to have you back. Man, can you believe that crazy stuff Assistant Chief Brittle did last week?"

"It's been a very weird week Mr. Swath. I can't say that I know exactly what it is you are talking about."

"Oh wow!" he exclaimed excitedly. "Didn't you hear about that wild fitness program he started? Four officers quit and two more were carried off by paramedics."

"What?!" Lloyd responded with genuine surprise "No, I hadn't heard about that one. I can't believe he actually tried to implement that while I was away."

"Well don't tell him you heard it from me Chief," Swath reminded with a wink. "It's just F.Y.U."

Canard stopped in his tracks and stared at Swath for a moment before blurting "What?!" with obvious suspicion. "What are you trying to say to me?"

Swath was a bit nervous that he may have upset the Chief, so he struggled momentarily as Canard watched his Adam's apple bounce up and down. "No...I mean, uhm...I only wanted to give you a heads up boss; you know, just an F.Y.U."

Lloyd remained quiet for a moment as he tried to work out whether this man was attempting to insult him.

Swath tried to change the subject. "We were hearing rumors that you wouldn't be coming back at all boss."

"Yeah, I can guess where those began."

"Well I'm just glad you made it back in one piece boss" he schmoozed.

"Okay," he said glumly, "thanks for the info Nick."

Lloyd was fairly certain that Nick Swath was only confused, and had not actually been trying to insult him with that misstated acronym 'F.Y.U.' comment. The guy was way too much of an insecure, brown-nosing snitch to be intentionally trying to get on his bad side. Although in the face of rumors that the Chief's days at Bitewoody were numbered, he could be trying to play both sides of the fence.

Finally back in his office, he sat alone in quiet vigil with his thoughts. As he sunk further into a caffeine-deficient funk, a shadow fell across his doorway. This one was from the unscheduled, yet oddly unsurprising arrival of Detective Abel Fleenor. 'Sure, why not,' Lloyd thought. As if he was incapable of torturing himself sufficiently, why not send in another radical element to add to his torment. When it rained, it poured. A flood of bad thoughts and negative emotions surged through Canard at the sight of this obnoxious man, yet his first reaction was much less confrontational.

"Detective Fleenor, of course, you're right on time" Canard kowtowed with a practiced fake authenticity. "Grab yourself a large cup of freshly brewed mud and pull up a chair."

Fleenor stared quietly, waiting for the punch line that never followed. When it didn't, he responded, "Thanks," and helped himself to a cup of the dark, aromatic water. To return the courtesy, Abel offered, "May I top off your cup for you?"

"Oh no!" he responded almost too adamantly. He curtailed his animation and explained, "It's just that I've recently learned about some coffee-related health issues and I'm trying to cut back on that stuff."

Fleenor raised an eyebrow in silent question as to why someone with the intention of abstaining would have a full pot so conveniently and tortuously near his office door. But that was not the reason the detective had stopped by Canard's office, so he quickly brushed that concern aside. Not wanting to waste time, he announced, "I still have several questions for you Mr. Canard."

"That's *Chief* Canard."

"Oh, well Chief Canard then" relented Fleenor.

He did that just to screw with Fleenor. It served to both break his rhythm and belittle him, as 'chief' was higher than 'detective' in police hierarchy. When the questioning began, Lloyd instinctively resorted to single word responses intended to supply only the vaguest appearance to an answer. The detective recognized this tactic from dozens of interviews with lifelong criminals. Abel had no doubt now that this man was a seasoned veteran of the underworld. The fact was, Canard made no conscious effort to misdirect the detective's inquiry. He had simply reverted to the method which he had adopted from years of interrogation by his wife: short, direct, single word responses, providing no details and volunteering no additional information. He really couldn't have offered much help anyway because he was sincerely baffled by the implications of the entire line of questioning. Canard had neither a clue about what the detective was really after nor what he was suspected of being involved in. He very clearly recalled their earlier encounter in the hospital when the detective ridiculously forbade him to speak. So he decided that since that's how this bumbling fool conducts an investigation, then he was going to comply, follow his lead, and make him work for every little bit of information.

"I simply want to know how you just happened to be on a plane that suffered mechanical problems" asked Detective Fleenor in a very accusatory tone.

"I don't believe it *just* happened."

"Well, would you kindly explain what you mean by that statement?"

"Whheeew!" sighed Lloyd loudly. "Haven't you figured this out yet detective?"

"Oh I have it figured out perfectly" rebounded Fleenor. "I know that you were behind it all, I just need your confession to complete the process Mr., uhm, Chief Canard."

"Actually, it was the landing gear detective."

"Aha!" exclaimed Fleenor, at the same time jamming his finger accusatorily in Canard's face. "How did you know that if you were not involved in the plot?"

"The problem with the landing gear was on the news; and *plot*?" he asked incredulously, "Good God man how could I have possibly managed that?"

"Why don't you tell me how you did it?" countered Fleenor superiorly.

"Well, seeing as the landing gear is outside the plane and I was sitting rather uncomfortably inside it, I don't think that any explanation I could give you, or that your wild imagination could possibly invent, would ever be able to convince anyone but you that I had managed to somehow tamper with it!" exclaimed Lloyd excitedly as he ran out of air in the long process.

"I sense your tension Canard. The jig is up man, give me all the details!"

"I don't doubt you may sense more than a little tension from me, because you appear to have honed your skills in this area to an incredible level of sensitivity." Canard was worked up and continued on a roll. "You, Detective Fleenor are probably more tense than a tuning fork. I can actually hear you humming as you attempt to collect nonexistent facts to connect the ridiculous clues your mind has determined must exist even without the most miniscule shred of genuine evidence. Quite obviously you cannot perform proper police work and employ your reasoning and logic skills to deduce facts from available clues. Instead, you seem to prefer working more like an author of fictitious detective novels and perform the operation in reverse where you have your predetermined outcome and then work backwards in the expectation that you must be able to find a path which leads from your preemptive conclusion regarding some imagined crime. Based on a simple missing person report, you ultimately designed an entirely fabricated scheme to find me guilty of offenses that were never actually perpetrated. In your little mind, I was unimpeachably guilty of being an animal-hating madman with a terroristic mindset and an apparent death wish. You, *detective,* were completely prepared to condemn me without investigation, trial or even the least minimal facts to support your outlandish allegations!"

"But I know you must know more than you are letting on" Fleenor insisted. "And I promise you that I will not stop until I find out who helped you sabotage that jetliner!"

"Oh you'd be surprised at just how little I actually know about what's been going on this past week" Canard retorted. "I am slowly finding out just how much effort has been put into discrediting me and undermining my authority by certain individuals during my brief absence."

"Detective Fleenor, let me make it completely clear that while I had no intention of being on an aircraft destined to suffer mechanical failure, I do not believe that my presence there was any sort of random coincidence. While I had absolutely no chance of picking the correct numbers for the lottery jackpot, it was almost inevitable that I would be there; on that exact plane, in that very predicament."

"Okay, now we're getting somewhere," said Fleenor with interest. "Please continue."

"I don't believe there is any more to say."

"As a matter of fact there is," countered Fleenor, "you can tell me who put you there."

"I really don't know that I can answer that one detective."

"And why not? Have you or your family been threatened? You know, if you are willing to work with me, then I can assure you we have the resources available to protect you" Fleenor offered.

"Is that right?" he laughed.

"Yes it is. Absolutely" promised the detective, feeling sure he was on the verge of a breakthrough.

The room was silent as the two men stared at each other; Fleenor thinking of the recognition he'd receive for identifying a terrorist cell, and Canard staring back, wondering how someone with such excessive imagination and limited intelligence could have possibly risen to the level of detective. 'Hell,' Lloyd mused, 'maybe the department would hire Perla.' She'd certainly fit right in with the witless imbecile sitting across the desk from him this morning.

"Okay?" prodded Fleenor reassuringly.

"Okay" repeated Lloyd in a bland tone, totally void of both emotion and comprehension.

Silence: except for the sound of Fleenor's well-worn soles scrapping across the unswept tile floor as he leaned forward in his chair imploring, "Give me a name!"

"God" whispered Lloyd conspiratorially as he too leant forward towards his interrogator.

Detective Fleenor clenched his teeth and dug his fingers into his own thigh before slowly repeating, "God."

"Of course," explained Canard, sitting back more comfortably as he saw the look of triumph and superiority flow from Fleenor's face, "or whatever you might choose to call him, her, it or even them for that matter. I have no idea what he, she, it or they have in mind by arranging these odd puzzles, but I am most adamantly certain that a merely random universe could not possibly be so chaotically tilted against a single human being by mere chance."

Fleenor's jaw dropped and his head hung lower as Lloyd took a deep breath and continued his thoughtful rant, "We cannot possibly imagine that all of this chaos in life is by any chance just accidental. If that were the case, wouldn't it be reasonable to assume that the bedlam was more evenly spread around to include more people?  I mean, why do you think that you and I keep meeting in ridiculously unexplainable situations like this?"

The detective didn't have an answer.  He felt certain that this sadistic man had it in for him.  He also wondered why whatever overseeing force might be manipulating them like such pawns had felt obliged to curse him with the persistent plague of Canard.  Abel certainly didn't feel he deserved it, but just couldn't imagine how to get rid of this scourge.

With Fleenor at a loss for words, Lloyd's pensive mood gave him a feeling of power and he continued expounding his random, reflective thoughts uninterrupted.  As Canard elaborated on his philosophical views, which the detective's feeble brain could not possibly grasp, Abel's mind drifted away from that cramped, stale little room.  His thoughts were on the imploding of his career that he could easily predict from further dealings with this particularly reprehensible character.  The department's decision makers would definitely not think much of him expending so many resources and producing so little results.  Fleenor was hurt, but not beaten.  Although he realized that Canard was correct in his assumptions, and he admittedly felt a twinge of embarrassment at his poor police work, he refused to admit these weaknesses in the face of this horrible, self-righteous man.  Abel still had his illogical equation of superiority to keep him going.  He felt comfortable that as he was still the investigator and Canard was still the principal suspect, the hierarchy of their current positions in this situation meant that the law would allow him to continue his unrestrained pursuit of an otherwise innocent man.  Besides, the legal system was designed to offer blind justice to its citizens and Fleenor was certain that his methods were fully reflective of that.  Since each of his moves in this game had been thoroughly unplanned, he was certain that he had adhered to the 'blind' requirement.  He had both the will and the sincere desire to persist in the interrogation, but he felt that horrible rumble in his bowels once again.  The detective excused himself and made a beeline for the lobby.  Lloyd said nothing, but displayed a sly smile.  He felt it was his brutal appraisal of the detective's ability that prompted his departure.

Abel made it to the lobby restroom and found no toilet seat covers.  "Damn that idiot Gonzalo!" he cursed, assuming the insane officer was the culprit.  Short on time, Fleenor quickly removed his jacket, hung it over the door and plopped down on the seat. He closed his eyes and arched his back as the tsunami of relief rushed over him. As he created his own minor explosion in the semi-privacy of a stall, the detective finally put together his first successful puzzle. By matching clues to evidence he determined that there was something about the coffee in Canard's office which had upset his stomach on both occasions. When he opened his eyes he saw something on the floor at his feet. He wasn't in the habit of picking things up off the bathroom floor, but the small item looked oddly familiar. Sure enough it was the fish he'd placed in his pocket several days before. The evidence bag was melted and the fish thoroughly flattened after having been dry cleaned and pressed.

Standing at the sink to wash his hands, Fleenor realized he was still holding the plastic bag. There was absolutely no need to keep it so he struggled to pry open the melted plastic. His efforts rustling the baggie drew the interest of a couple Bitewoody employees who were also in the restroom. They watched the stranger closely, expecting to witness a junkie addressing his fix. Instead they saw the stranger remove a small, red fish from a worn, damaged bag. Whatever this guy was addicted to it was something they'd never heard of, but his actions held their undivided attention.

Lost in his own thoughts, Fleenor never noticed that he was being watched so closely as he removed the dead fish from the plastic bag. Shaking his head in disbelief at all that had happened, he turned from the sink and returned to the stall where he dropped the tiny, well-pressed carcass into the bowl and kicked the handle with his left foot to send it unceremoniously on its way.

The two witnesses shared a glance of disgusted surprise at what they'd just seen and shouted simultaneously at the man exiting the stall, "Hey, what are you doing?!" Fleenor jumped at the sudden noise. He was so bewildered by the next accusation of, "You killer!" that he looked around to see who the men could possibly be addressing. Seeing no one else in the room, he quickly surmised that the two scowling men were directing their angry taunts at him. Before he could commence an explanation, one of the men exclaimed, "We saw what you did to that little fishy!"

Fleenor was caught off guard by both their presence and their fury, but most of all by the fact that he'd just heard a grown man use the childish term 'fishy.' Having become well versed in reading body language, Abel could see that these two men were feeding off each other's anger. The hostility showing in their posture clearly indicated their intention to seek revenge for the life of the fish they mistakenly thought had just been murdered right before their eyes. Aware of the way these people were prone to overreact from Mr. Canard's recent experiences, Fleenor judged that his best option was to run for the door. He exited the restroom and picked up the pace to traverse the expansive lobby. Looking back to find the location of his pursuers, he barely missed hitting the blind gentleman who had just completed his business in the Union Bank and was now rounding the corner into the lobby. He did not miss the disabled customer's guide dog. Fleenor's right knee rammed solidly into the rib cage of the service animal. This caused the canine to emit a loud yip of pain, which in turn drew the attention of everyone in the area just as the detective was stumbling over its fallen body. The blind man lost hold of the leash and was thrown backwards by the force from Abel's flailing right arm. Abel stumbled flagrantly all the way to the front door where he grabbed the handle to steady himself, then made a quick look at the mess he'd left behind. The men from the restroom were yelling at him, but their din was largely muted by the other people screaming additional threats at him for having trampled the Seeing Eye dog. Now a security officer and three other men from the lobby joined the chase after Detective Fleenor as he ran out the door. Another seven people dropped to their knees surrounding the poor dog, as the blind man lay moaning and unnoticed in a bright red puddle of blood where his head had struck the tile floor. Abel beat feet to his car with the purposeful intention of never looked back at that crazy place again.

* * * *

In the end there were no charges filed against Canard. Even with the grand efforts of several bungling police officers, he was revealed only as the innocent recipient of excessive bad luck. Although each crazy incident had its corresponding explanation, the lore of Lloyd Canard's antics remained alive in the B.E.O.T.C.H. rumor mill. His legendary murder of an innocent cat; unprovoked assaults on women and small animals; multiple arrests in New

York; and (thanks to Gonzalo's cousin) the story of the misunderstanding at the Fort Lauderdale Airport security checkpoint were all repeated infinitely.

The autopsy performed on the cat (yes, they did actually go through with it) revealed that it had been killed in a hit and run several days prior to Gonzalo's attempt to resuscitate it. Assistant Chief Russell Brittle's investigation lay dormant and the assailant was as of yet unidentified. He refused to consider the case unsolvable or even irrelevant and dedicated a good deal of time every day to studying his notes on it. Lloyd thought it was a pretty idiotic pursuit, but since it did cut down the amount of time Russell pestered him with other stupid ideas he was happy to let his assistant continue to waste time on it.

* * * *

Fleenor reluctantly closed the case on Lloyd Canard, but was silently determined to keep his eye on this man. Officially the case was archived as 'solved' since Abel did eventually discover the whereabouts of the reported missing person. In the feeble mind of the great Detective Fleenor, this suspicious character was still a prime suspect in a grand plot as of yet undiscovered. The detective knew it was only a matter of time before he'd stumble upon the right clue to break the case wide open.

* * * *

Lloyd was home and uninjured. Everything was back to normal; which was not really any improvement, but at least he wasn't in jail or hospital at the moment. He settled back into his usual zone of discomfort and misfortune. As he removed his work clothes to get more comfortable in a tank top and shorts, Perla chattered away in the background.

"An I forgit to tell you I go to hospital too" she almost bragged.

"What?! When?!" he blurted with a streak of fear that she'd next tell him that she was pregnant.

"While ju were making trouble at New Jork."

"Well what happened?"

"I get sick," Perla explained, "but lucky I not really sick because dat doctor was no gud."

"Yeah?" he responded; calmer now and beginning to return to his normal state of less-than-half listening.

"He waste my time," she continued, "he don know nuthin' about medicine I think."

"Yeah?" droned Lloyd. His mind was already galloping off in another direction.

"Da doctor try to tell me I have a bad diet, but I tell him I don even do any diet!" she exclaimed triumphantly.

He had a clue what the doctor must have been trying to convey, but out of self interest he chose to keep it to himself. It was much easier to shake his head and laugh at the doctor who wasn't here than to do the doctor's job and tell Perla she needed to ease up on the inhalation of marshmallows and lose some weight. If the doctor hadn't successfully explained this message to the patient then it certainly wasn't the husbands place to step in and assume to know what he'd meant to convey. Besides, he had to live here and the doctor might be lucky enough to never have to see her again.

He wanted to wash up first, and then he'd probably have a cold can of black beans for dinner. Heating it up would be simple and quick, but based on principle alone, he never seriously considered doing such a thing. Once a Marine always a Marine; he'd eat his beans cold to ensure he didn't become soft and spoiled. At least that's what he told himself.

Andi walked by the open bathroom door and paused to observe her father contort himself in an attempt to squeeze his shoulder underneath the sink faucet.

Seeing her, he called, "Hi Andi, how was school?"

"I dunno" his daughter answered.

Unperturbed by her lack of interest, he continued, "Well, it's nice to be back home anyway."

"Did you go somewhere?" Andi inquired.

Lloyd stared at his daughter and wondered how she could have missed out on all the recent excitement. He realized that a teenager's mind and body rarely reside at the same address, so he simply answered, "No...not really sweetie," then resumed washing his armpit in the sink.

Andi stared at her father as if he were an alien with his weird insistence on bathing in the sink. She really had no clue how this odd old man could possibly be her real father. Without another word Andi shook her head, rolled her eyes and huffed in disgust as she walked away with the arduous air of average adolescent angst.

Back in the kitchen, his eyes caught sight of a long string of ants across the kitchen counter. He followed it and found that it stretched to the wall, down the cabinet, along the floor and underneath a crack by the back door. He assumed that they must have been conducting some form of survival training for the colony's elite force of scout ants, as they were sure to have had a hard time finding the scent of anything to eat in this underused kitchen. The oven hadn't been fired up in months, and since Perla never spent any time in here, there would not even be any marshmallow crumbs lying around. It struck him that maybe he should take their example as a sign that he too needed to make an escape. Instead, he turned his attention away from the retreating march of ants, filled his tumbler with ice and grabbed his old pal Scottie by the neck.

He settled in his La-Z-Boy recliner with his can of black beans and a flimsy plastic spoon, watching television and letting his mind drift elsewhere. He considered that his life might not be as bad as he sometimes saw it. Perla wasn't the worst possible spouse he could imagine being burdened with. At least she was usually home rather than running around in the street, or acting like a loony extremist at some conference snatching hotdogs from strangers. She had a sharp eye for doo-doo but she was discreet enough to keep that fetish in house. In his opinion, she enjoyed shopping way too much, but Perla really did have a knack for finding things on sale; even though most of it was absolutely useless stuff that was marked down because no one else would buy it. Andi wasn't a bad kid really, just a typical teenager. The chasm between them was nothing out of the ordinary for a father and teen daughter, and the phenomenon of their communication gap was simply a part of growing up.

In all honesty, a lesser man would have never been able to handle the aggravation of Canard's daily routine. The average guy would have wound up in jail for killing one of the idiots surrounding him, or would have completely lost his mind from the excessive strain of restraint. Sure the world would be a better place if people paid more attention to the reality of things happening around them: taking the time to fully comprehend the truth instead of jumping to faulty conclusions from every statement and event.  But what was the chance of that ever happening?  Lloyd knew he couldn't change the world and that the chance of it changing on its own was highly unlikely.  Even as he sat and pondered these questions he knew very well that these personal peeves were well beyond his ability to ever affect.  He knew that a man had to know his limitations, and stressing over things which you cannot possibly control was a sure way to make yourself sick.

Lloyd considered what changes might actually be within his realm of influence.  It was a very short and unimpressive list.  He contemplated making his first attempt at changing his life by skipping the Scotch tonight.  On the other hand, he realized the fact that the two biggest parts of his usual diet were coffee and Scotch.  Had the liquor acted as medicine in preventing him getting sick from Jordan's toilet coffee?  Maybe the alcohol had killed some of the crap in his system from the daily consumption of a bacterially burdened beverage.  He reasoned that if the Scotch was possibly of some medicinal benefit then maybe he'd better not stop drinking so abruptly.  It would probably be best to ensure all that contaminated coffee had been thoroughly flushed through his liver before making a change that could be detrimental to his health.  Looking at the bottle with even more respect than usual, Lloyd decided that he'd pour just one.

## Also by Adam Kirk Pruden

## Relationslips: Definitely NOT A Dating Guide

Most people have a couple stories about bad dates and failed relationships, but most people are not stupid enough to publish their experiences for the entire world to read. Here lie the bare revelations of one man's failures at meeting, dating and developing successful relationships with women.

"My last boyfriend used to tie me up, gag me and get pretty rough. I left him after six years because I felt he didn't respect me." Christina revealed to me on our second date.

"I was afraid it would scare you away if you knew about the amputation" Ilene apologized on our first meeting.

"Now that we are dating I expect you to be a real man and start paying some of my bills: Maybe my car payment or the rent" Marie explained to me on our second date.

I picked up a Bible and began reading verses of interest quietly to the young boy seated next to me. Yuni surprised the entire room by jumping up and yelling "Stop whispering things about me!"

"I didn't mean to lead you on by giving you my number" Kassie cautioned me when I called the number she had given me.

"You breathe too much" my loving wife stated.

http://www.RelationslipsBook.com